THE WITCH
OF
TURLINGHAM
ACADEMY

THE WITCH
OF
TURLINGHAM
ACADEMY

ELLIE BOSWELL

www.atombooks.net/tween

ATOM

First published in Great Britain in 2012 by Atom
Reprinted 2012 (twice), 2013 (twice)

Copyright © 2012 by Working Partners

The moral right of the author has been asserted.

A CIP catalogue record for this book
is available from the British Library.

ISBN 978-1-907410-95-6

Typeset in Minion by M Rules
Printed and bound in Great Britain by
Clays Ltd, St Ives plc

Papers used by Atom are from well-managed forests
and other responsible sources.

MIX
Paper from
responsible sources
FSC® C104740

Atom
An imprint of
Little, Brown Book Group
100 Victoria Embankment
London EC4Y 0DY

An Hachette UK Company
www.hachette.co.uk

www.atombooks.net

With special thanks to Leila Rasheed

ONE

Sophie peered round the stone pillar. She beckoned to the tall, curly-haired boy who was trying, not very successfully, to conceal himself behind the opposite pillar.

'Come on, Callum!' she hissed. She ducked out from her hiding place and ran on tiptoe down the corridor, dodging from sunlight to shadow as she passed the tall windows. Behind her, she heard a clatter and glanced round to see Callum's arms fly out as he stumbled.

He quickly recovered. 'We haven't all got your dainty feet,' he said as he caught up with her.

Sophie giggled. 'Sorry! That tile's been loose for ever, I thought you knew about it.'

'Nope. Not all of us spend our free time memorising every single tile in the school.' As they ran down the corridor side by side, he added, 'You haven't even told me what the welcome back prank is yet – it better be good after all this!'

'Don't worry,' said Sophie with a grin. 'It will be!'

Footsteps echoed down the corridor, and Sophie skidded to a halt.

'Uh-oh. Sounds like a teacher, hide!'

'Where?'

Sophie pushed him towards a display case containing the enormous silver Turlingham Academy Hockey Cup. They were barely behind it when the double doors at the end of the corridor burst open and a tall, thin woman with a sharp face came hurrying through. Sophie held her breath and exchanged a horrified glance with Callum. But the woman swished past without a glance, her smart shoes tapping out a no-

nonsense beat. She pushed the next set of double doors and was on her way, leaving them swinging and squeaking behind her.

Sophie reeled out from behind the case, clutching her heart in mock collapse. 'It had to be Mrs Freeman! Can you imagine if she'd caught us?' she wondered, making sure to keep her voice low.

'Yeah, gruel and solitary confinement for the rest of the year.' Callum grinned. 'What's she doing here anyway? I thought you said all the teachers were in a meeting?'

'Who knows – maybe she forgot her broomstick.'

They ran on, laughing quietly.

'Here we are!' Sophie came to a halt in front of a big oak door. A brass panel next to it read: TAMSIN MORROW, HEADMISTRESS.

Callum tried the handle.

'Locked.' He sighed.

'Not a problem.' Sophie reached up towards the top ledge of the door frame and jumped. Her fingers knocked something small and metal and the key skidded off the top. Callum caught it and handed it to her.

'Nice work,' he said, nodding in appreciation.

Sophie shrugged as she turned the key in the lock. 'Mum's accidentally locked herself out of her office so many times I suggested she should hide a spare key up here!'

She opened the door and stepped inside.

Behind her, Callum gasped sharply. 'Um, hello, Mrs Freeman!'

Sophie whirled round, her heart beating fast. She saw Callum grinning at her . . . and no one else.

'That was *not* funny!' she said, and whacked him lightly on the arm.

'Should've seen your face!'

Sophie shut the door and they leaned against it, holding their sides as they laughed. Portraits of previous headmistresses glared down from the walls. Callum's laughter died away.

'Wow, those aren't the posters I'd want in my room,' he said, grimacing as he gazed from one painting to the next. 'They're even scarier than the old headmasters in Dad's office. Don't they freak you out?'

Sophie shrugged. 'I grew up here, remember? They

4

feel like relatives.' She started opening the drawers of the filing cabinets.

'Okaaaay. Remind me never to come to your family reunions.' Callum shook his head as if to get rid of the image. 'So, what are we looking for?'

'Aha!' Sophie found exactly what they'd come for and picked up the cream squares of thick paper. 'Blank report cards.'

She handed a pile to Callum.

'Now what?'

Sophie grinned at his puzzled expression.

'Now you use your imagination and your in-depth knowledge of your friends.'

'Um, right.' Callum looked dubious.

'Thing about reports,' said Sophie cheerfully, as she perched on her mother's desk and started writing, 'is they talk about all the wrong stuff. I mean, who cares that Erin Best is no good at History? In the really important subject of Gossip, however, she gets an A-plus.'

'I get it.' Callum smiled.

'And for Daydreaming About Boys, she gets an A.

All her practising is definitely paying off!' Sophie filled in the report card as she spoke.

'This is going to be fun,' Callum said, grabbing a pen.

'Told you!' Sophie said.

They both worked in silence for a few minutes. Sophie tried to fill one in for as many of her friends as possible but was interrupted when Callum handed her a card. Sophie saw her own name – and also a very familiar one: Jareth Quinn. His movie posters were the ones that covered the walls in her room.

'Sophie Morrow – A for Celebrity Crushes,' she read aloud. 'An *A*? I'm not *that* into Jareth Quinn,' she protested, going red.

'Think yourself lucky, I was going to give you an A-plus with distinction for extra effort!' Callum looked down at the desk. 'Hey, have we run out of report cards already? I've still got a couple to go.'

Sophie got up and peered back into the filing cabinet, but it was empty. 'None left in here. I'll check the desk drawers; you have a look in those piles of paper on the windowsill.'

She opened the top drawer and quickly searched through, finding nothing but scrap paper, pens and paper clips. She glanced at her watch. It was nearly eleven.

'Hurry, Callum, they'll be out of their meeting any minute.' She opened the next one down. It was full of rubber bands, staples and Post-it notes. She pushed it shut and opened the bottom drawer. Inside was a stack of yellowing papers. Sophie grinned: her mother clearly didn't tidy her desk very often! She felt a twinge of guilt for going through her mother's things, but then remembered – term couldn't possibly begin without one of her legendary pranks! She pushed the papers aside. Right at the bottom of the drawer her hand closed on something firm and rectangular.

It was a package, wrapped in brown paper and string. As she lifted it out, her gaze fell on the address label. Even though the blue ink had faded to grey, she could still make out the firm, spiky handwriting. It read:

Miss Sophie Morrow
Turlingham Academy
Norfolk

Sophie's mouth fell open. The package was addressed to her. So what was it doing in her mum's desk?

'Callum,' she said.

Callum turned round.

'Look at this.' She held it up to him.

Callum came over and took the box from her, turning it upside down and around. He frowned. 'Check out the date,' he said, pointing out the postmark as he handed it back.

Sophie did some quick maths.

'Posted five years ago.' She shook it gently. Something rattled inside. 'It's still sealed. Do you think I should open it?'

'Why not? It's addressed to you.'

Sophie hesitated, still unsure. Sneaking into her mum's office for a practical joke was one thing; uncovering secrets was another. But the package had been *meant* for her.

'Oh go on, open it,' Callum said. 'I'm curious now.'

Sophie unpicked the Sellotape. It was so old that the tape had turned yellow and the glue had dried up. When she opened the wrapping a plain white card fell out on to the floor. Callum picked it up.

'For Sophie on her thirteenth birthday,' he read. 'No name.'

'How weird! My thirteenth birthday was months ago – why do you think Mum didn't give it to me then?'

'Maybe she forgot, it was sent years ago.' Callum craned his neck for another look at the box. 'Do you recognise the handwriting?'

'Not at all. It might say who it's from inside.' She slowly lifted the lid of the box, her heartbeat quickening. Presents were exciting at the best of times, but a present from an anonymous sender ... She knew she'd better open it quickly, or they'd risk getting caught.

Inside was a silver ring, with a stone shaped like a crescent moon. The stone was a milky white colour and it seemed to glow with a delicate, strange light –

almost as if there was moonshine trapped inside. Her face broke into a smile. 'Oh, wow – it's beautiful!'

'Jewellery,' said Callum, sounding disappointed. He turned away. 'I'll look for more report cards.'

'It's totally gorgeous!' Sophie stared at the ring, then lifted it out of the box and slowly slipped it on to her index finger. It fitted. Perfectly. So perfectly that it gave her goosebumps. She shivered. It was *more* than goosebumps. It was like electric tingles running all over her skin.

'Whoever got me this is really, really good at choosing presents,' she said. 'Callum – who do you think it could be? Who could have sent it to me?'

Callum hesitated as he bent over the pile of papers. 'Well, there is one obvious possibility,' he said, not looking up.

For a moment Sophie couldn't think what he meant.

'Oh,' she said. 'My dad?'

'Well – yeah.'

Sophie hesitated. She didn't like to think about her dad. He'd been gone since she was three – just walked out without a word of explanation. *Do I want it to be from him?* she wondered. *Or not?*

'I doubt it,' she said, trying to keep her tone light. 'Why would he send a present after all this time? And why for my thirteenth birthday?'

'Well, who else could it be?'

Sophie bit her lip. In the silence she heard footsteps heading towards them, down the corridor, stopping outside the door. Sophie and Callum stared at each other.

'Quick,' gasped Callum. 'Hide the evidence!'

He threw the report cards into Sophie's bag. She shoved the empty box back into the drawer, pulling bits of Sellotape off her fingers, and, after two tries, managed to shut the drawer. The door handle was turning. She glanced around the room. There was nowhere to hide! They hadn't planned this properly at all. As the door opened, Sophie pushed her hands into her pockets to conceal the ring. A shadow loomed. Sophie just had time to hope it wasn't her mum, and *really* hope it wasn't Mrs Freeman.

As the figure stepped into the light she could see it

was neither of them. It was worse. Sophie couldn't help a groan escaping.

'You two are in *so* much trouble,' came a sneering voice.

It was Maggie Millar – the Head Prefect.

TWO

Maggie blocked the doorway, a triumphant smirk on her face. Sophie briefly considered the possibility of dodging round her and escaping, but another look at the Head Prefect's face convinced her not to try it. Maggie was the captain of the hockey team and a lot stronger than she looked.

'Maggie, it's so nice to see you back so ... early,' Sophie said with a smile pasted on her face.

Maggie looked at her with disgust. 'I knew you'd

be playing one of your pranks. This time I thought I'd catch you red-handed.'

'It's just a bit of fun, Maggie!' Callum said.

Sophie tried to make a 'Shhh!' face at him. Explaining never worked with Maggie Millar.

'Breaking into the headmistress's office? Is that just a bit of fun?'

'But—'

'No excuses. You're both coming with me!'

Sophie and Callum exchanged despairing glances as Maggie marched them down the corridor. There would be no getting out of this one.

Maggie pushed open the double doors to the hall and nodded Sophie and Callum forward. Sophie walked into the middle of the large space. Rows of plastic chairs had been laid out and every member of staff was there. Mr Pearce and Sophie's mum were up on the stage, leading the meeting. Mr Pearce saw them first and nudged Sophie's mum. Mrs Morrow broke off mid-sentence as she met Sophie's eyes.

'Sophie!' she exclaimed. 'What on earth—?'

Sophie could feel herself going bright red with embarrassment as chairs scraped and the other teachers turned round. A hundred pairs of eyes stared at them.

'Mrs Morrow, Mr Pearce, I'm so sorry to disturb you,' Maggie interrupted, batting her eyelids. 'I know you have such a lot to prepare for the new school term but I thought you should know ... ' She paused, waiting for the attention of the whole faculty. 'I caught these two burgling Mrs Morrow's office. They'd let themselves in.' Maggie hid a smile as a chorus of gasps greeted her announcement.

Mrs Freeman sat up straight as a stick, her lips pursed and frowning deeply.

'We weren't burgling!' Callum insisted.

'Callum Pearce, silence!' Mrs Freeman snapped. 'Maggie, thank you. You are impressively vigilant – and it isn't even term time yet.'

'A true Head Prefect is never off duty,' said Maggie, dipping her head in fake modesty.

Mrs Freeman turned to Mr Pearce and Mrs Morrow. 'As joint heads of this school, I'm sure you will be keen to punish these pupils severely, even though they *are* your children.'

'Of course,' said Sophie's mum, frowning at what Mrs Freeman was implying. 'Sophie has never had any special treatment, and I'm sure that Callum hasn't, either.' She turned to Sophie. 'Sophie, what on earth were you thinking? Term hasn't even started yet, and you're already breaking the rules. Can't you see how badly this reflects on you?'

Sophie *could* see, and she felt awful for showing her mum up in front of her staff. She hung her head. 'I'm really sorry, Mum – I mean, Mrs Morrow.'

'And Callum, I'm very disappointed in you,' Mr Pearce added. 'As the headmaster's son, you should be setting a good example.'

Callum mumbled an apology.

'What were you doing in there?' Sophie's mother asked. 'You had absolutely no right to go into my office.'

'We were getting report cards. We were—'

'Forging reports!' said Mrs Freeman. 'Maggie, make a note of this.'

Maggie whisked a little red notebook and a pen from her pocket and began writing.

'It was just a joke.' Sophie pulled a handful of the cards from her bag, walked up to the stage and offered them to her mother.

Mrs Morrow took the cards and turned them over in her hand.

She read them to herself, then read aloud. 'Pupil: Erin Best. Subject: Gossip. Grade: A-plus.' Sophie cringed, they sounded a bit stupid read out in front of the teachers. Her mum read on. 'Subject: Day-dreaming About Boys. Grade: A.'

There was some sniggering from the teachers at the back. Mrs Freeman whipped round, looking annoyed. 'This is no laughing matter!' she said.

Her mum read the next card. 'Pupil: Kaz Fahmy. Subject: Fancying Callum Pearce. Grade: A-plus, top of the class!' Mrs Morrow raised her eyebrows at Callum. 'Callum, is this true?'

'No, totally not,' he muttered, going bright red and shuffling his feet.

'Oh, but it is,' contributed Mr Powell, the

Geography teacher. 'If the notes she and Joanna Grey pass to each other in my class are anything to go by.'

The teachers all laughed, and even Sophie's mum smiled.

'Pupil: Mark Little. Subject: Hair Gel Gymnastics. Grade: B-plus.'

'I object!' called Mr McGowan, the History teacher. 'The boy deserves an A-minus at least!'

Other teachers laughed and Sophie stifled a giggle.

Her mum read out the last card. 'Pupil: Sophie Morrow. Subject: Celebrity Crushes. Grade: A.' She looked at Sophie and couldn't stop herself from smiling, but she wagged her finger. 'And an F for Rule Keeping. It's a harmless joke, so I'll let it go this time,' she said, handing the cards back. 'But if you ever want to take something from my office again, you must ask, OK?'

Sophie nodded in relief. She thought of the ring, still on her finger, and felt a pang of guilt. But now hardly seemed like the best time to discuss it.

'Thanks, Mu—Mrs Morrow.' She looked around at the teachers. 'And we're really sorry for causing trouble – we didn't mean to.'

Callum echoed her. 'Yeah, we're really sorry.'

As they walked out of the hall, Callum whispered to her, 'Did you see the look on Maggie Millar's face when we were let off the hook? She was fuming. You'd better steer clear of her this term, Soph!'

She intended to do just that.

Sophie smiled to herself as she placed the last report card on Lauren's bed. She glanced out of the window, enjoying the fresh sea smell and the sound of the waves beating against the nearby cliffs. Down in the car park, a coach had arrived. Some of her Year 9 friends were already getting off it.

'Brilliant!' Sophie ran out of the dorm, down the big stone staircase to the entrance hall, and out into the courtyard. Girls in Turlingham's red and grey uniform were unloading their suitcases, laughing and talking and greeting their friends.

'Erin, Lauren!' Sophie dashed through the crowd and flung her arms around her best friends. Erin's green eyes glittered with pleasure as she hugged her back, and little Lauren O'Connor joined in the hug.

'It's so good to see you again!' Sophie exclaimed. 'It's been . . .'

'Only two weeks.' Lauren laughed. 'You were over at mine in August!'

'Yeah, but way longer for me!' Erin protested. 'Texting every morning just isn't the same.'

'How was your flight, Erin?' Sophie asked.

'Boring! It's, like, eleven hours from LAX and there were no cute boys on the plane.' They linked arms and walked towards the main school building together. 'But oh, girls, wait till you see the new photos of Bugsy.' Erin flipped open her phone and Sophie and Lauren craned over, cooing at the pictures of the black Labrador puppy. 'He's sooo adorable – the best thirteenth birthday present ever!'

Suddenly Sophie was grabbed from behind by four arms. She beamed as she heard a familiar loud laugh, echoed by a timid giggle. 'Hey, Kaz, Joanna!' She turned round and hugged them.

'Hey, girls, good to be back!' Kaz said. Sophie opened her mouth to reply, but Kaz hadn't finished. 'Listen, I've such a cool idea for tonight.' She pulled

Joanna and Lauren towards her, and beckoned the others in as she whispered, 'A midnight feast!'

'Ooh!' Joanna gasped. 'I've brought a bag of my mum's cookies.'

'The famous double chocolate chip ones?' Kaz said in delight. 'Jo, you're a star!'

'Awesome idea!' agreed Erin. 'Where can we have it? The big linen cupboard on the Year 7 floor?'

Sophie dropped behind as the others chattered happily. The feast sounded amazing, but at midnight she'd be away from all the action – at home in bed. As the head teacher's daughter, she shared her mum's private quarters rather than sleeping in the dorms with everyone else. She tried to look forward to hearing all about the midnight feast the next day, but it wasn't easy. *I wish I could be with my friends all the time.* It was hard not to feel left out.

'That sounds like so much fun,' Sophie said, not meaning to speak aloud.

Erin turned round. 'Soph! I forgot . . .'

'There must be some way you can come along,' said Lauren, scrunching up her face.

'Have you ever asked your mum if she'd let you stay in the dorms?' asked Kaz. 'Just for a night?'

'It's worth a try,' Sophie agreed.

She raced over to her mother, who was walking across the courtyard towards her office.

'Muuuuum,' Sophie said, with a cheesy grin on her face.

'Uh-oh, I don't like the sound of this,' said her mum, eyebrows raised.

'Please can I stay in the dorms tonight? I want to be with my friends.'

'Oh, I see, so you can get a really good night's sleep and be rested in the morning for the first day of term,' her mother teased. 'Not so you can catch up on the gossip – of course not!'

'But I haven't seen them for ages,' Sophie said. 'If I get all my catching up done tonight, I'll be able to pay much more attention in lessons tomorrow, won't I?'

Her mother laughed. 'I don't know, Sophie. You've not exactly got off to a good start, have you?'

'I'll be good for the rest of the year, I promise.'

'Hmm, a likely story.' She glanced at her phone as it

vibrated with a text. 'Well, it's true I'm rushed off my feet at the moment. There are two new pupils arriving tomorrow – a brother and sister – and the gym equipment I ordered *still* hasn't arrived, if you can believe it.' She put her head on one side and looked at Sophie with a smile. 'On second thoughts, it might be nice to have you out of my hair for one evening.'

Sophie jumped up and down. 'Yes!'

'I'll have to check with Mrs Freeman about putting a mattress down, as head matron it's her decision really.'

'Oh, Mum, you might just as well say no,' Sophie groaned. 'Mrs Freeman hates me.'

'Don't be silly, of course she doesn't! I'll make a good case for you, anyway.' Her mum gave her a wink.

'Thanks, Mum.' Sophie gave her a grateful hug. 'You're the best!'

Sophie dashed back to her friends, smiling wickedly. 'I know an even better place than the linen cupboard – how about we have our feast in the old lighthouse? Callum and I finally worked out how to get into it over the summer.' She pointed up on the cliffs at the tall, red and white building that reared above the school. 'We can get in and go right to the top, and . . . um . . . do whatever you do at a midnight feast.'

'Eat chocolate and talk about boys. *Duh*,' Erin chipped in, and everyone burst out laughing.

The dorm was absolutely silent, but Sophie knew that everyone else was just as awake as she was. She glanced at her alarm clock's glowing face: almost feast time! Mrs Freeman had turned out the lights ages ago, and she must have returned to her own room by now.

Sophie realised something was shining dimly in the dark room. The crescent moon ring. It was still on her finger.

I ought to take it back, she thought. Even though it had been meant for her, taking it felt like stealing. Deep inside, she knew that Callum was right – it was probably from her dad. She guessed that was why her mum had kept it from her.

Her memories of her dad were as patchy as a faded

old photo … but they were good memories. For a moment, she allowed herself to remember the nice things: her father's warm brown eyes, the sound of his laughter. But before she could get too soppy, she reminded herself that he'd just walked out on them: abandoned her and left her mum to cope alone.

Who needs a present from a dad like that? she thought. But perhaps he regretted leaving … perhaps that was why he had sent it? It was so puzzling that she sighed aloud.

'Sophie, that had better not be a yawn I just heard!' whispered Kaz, sitting up in bed. 'It's time to go!'

THREE

Sophie covered her mouth to stop herself giggling as she hid in the long shadows of the courtyard. Lauren and Joanna were behind her; Kaz and Erin were up ahead. Sophie saw Kaz turn and beckon them forward, and she ran, keeping to the gloom, across towards the Science lab. They made their way, single file, between the Science lab and the main school building, until they reached the fence that marked the school boundary. Beyond the fence was the cliff meadow, and the light-house rose from it, looming over them in the night.

Kaz pulled aside a loose plank in the fence and waved them through.

'After you, ladies! One at a time – it's a bit narrow.'

As Sophie waited her turn to squeeze through the gap, she hugged her hoodie closer around her. It was cold and there was a strong wind blowing in from the sea. She had a funny feeling that she was being watched. Her gaze lit on something white and spooky – the plastic skeleton from the Science lab, leaning against the window. She grinned and glanced up into the sky. Against the pale clouds, she saw a bird swooping. It passed close by her and she saw its hooked beak, black feathers and bright eyes. She felt a sudden shiver.

'What's up?' Erin turned to her.

'Oh, nothing. Just there's a raven up there.' She followed Erin through the gap in the fence, keeping in the shelter of the wall.

'A raven?' said Erin.

'Yeah,' Sophie replied. 'I've never seen one here before. Lots of seagulls, but never a raven.' But Erin was already running towards the lighthouse with the rest of the girls.

They piled up at the lighthouse door, Lauren bouncing with nervous excitement. Kaz tried the handle, then pushed.

'It's locked!' Her shoulders slumped. 'Is there another way in, Sophie?'

'It's all right, there's a knack to it. Let me.' Sophie stepped forward. 'You have to lift the handle – like this – and then shove it with your shoulder.'

The door flew open and Sophie stumbled inside. The room was pitch black, narrow and round, and the winding staircase rose above them, spiralling up to the lantern room.

'Yay for Sophie!' Kaz tapped her hands together in a quiet clap and the rest gave a whispered cheer.

Sophie curtsied then held the door open to let her friends in. Just in time, too – she pushed it shut as the rain hit the ground.

'Phew!' said Joanna, with a shiver. She pulled out her torch and passed it to Kaz. 'Here, Kaz, you take it – I'd rather not go first.'

'OK, everyone,' Kaz ordered, switching on the torch. 'Onwards and upwards!'

They followed Kaz up the winding stairs, their footsteps echoing and mingling with the sound of the wind battering at the strong walls. The thin beam of light from her torch picked out cobwebs and cracks.

'This is awesomely spooky!' Erin whispered as they climbed. 'But are you sure we won't get busted?'

'Yeah, does anyone ever come in here?' Lauren asked, sounding worried.

'No way,' Sophie told them. 'No one's come up here since the lantern stopped working, and that was about fifty years ago. That's what Mum says, anyway.'

She stopped speaking as she realised Lauren wasn't listening, but staring at her hand on the rickety bannister.

'Soph, I love your ring! Is it new?' Lauren reached up to touch the shining crescent moon.

'Um – yeah. I mean – no. Sort of.'

'*Sort of*?' Erin laughed as she stopped climbing to turn and look. 'What is it, a present from a secret admirer?'

'No!' Sophie laughed. 'I meant, I've had it for years, but I only just found it.' *Which is true enough*, she thought.

'Well, it's gorgeous,' said Lauren. 'I love the way it catches the moonlight.'

'Can I see?' Joanna leaned over.

'Your bracelet is nice, too, Erin,' said Sophie, wanting to change the subject. 'Where did you get it?'

Erin slipped the bracelet off with a proud smile. 'It's a family heirloom. Real gold.'

The girls gasped as they squeezed in to see, and Sophie quickly turned the ring around on her finger so the crescent moon wasn't showing. *I'll be putting it back in Mum's office soon anyway*, she told herself. *No point drawing attention to it.* Luckily the others were busy admiring Erin's bracelet.

'Yeah, it's been passed down for generations. My grandma gave it to me for my birthday. I really love it.' Erin put her bracelet back on and they continued to climb the stairs. 'The no jewellery rule totally sucks.' She shrugged. 'But I'll keep it in my bedside drawer and wear it when there are no teachers about.'

Kaz stopped as she realised they had finally reached the top of the stairs and a tiny door.

'This is it,' said Sophie. 'Just push.'

Kaz shoved the door open, and the distant noise of wind was suddenly much louder. Beyond were three more steps which led into a circular room about the size of Sophie's bedroom, but with walls made of glass. One by one the girls entered, Sophie last. She looked up to see the huge lantern looming above them, dominating the centre of the room. All around raindrops glistened and slithered, and the rain drummed fiercely on the glass.

'Whoa! This is so awesome,' Erin cried.

'Yeah! Amazing!' said Kaz, running to the edge of the room to look out. The others spread out, exploring. For a moment, Sophie heard only gasps of admiration as they took in the view: the black sea and sky on one side, and the moonlit gables and towers of the main school building on the other. Right below them were the modern additions to the school: the squat brick Science block and the new structure that housed the teachers' facilities and sick bay.

'I can see your house from here, Sophie!' Kaz pointed. Sophie went over and smiled to see her little cottage, nestling below the wing that housed the girls' dorms. The main school building looked spooky in the wind, like a huge bird hunched over with its wings spread out.

'Hey, you guys are looking at the lame bit!' Erin called from the other side of the glass room. 'I can see the boys' dorms!'

Giggling, they ran over to join her.

'Ooh, is that a light on?' said Lauren. 'I wonder who's awake?'

'It might be Mark Little,' said Erin, in such a lovestruck voice that they all burst out laughing.

'Let's flash him a message in Morse code!' suggested Kaz.

'I'll do it,' said Sophie, taking the torch from Kaz. She flashed it randomly out of the window. 'Erin – loves – Mark –'

'Sophie, nooo!' Erin dived to grab the torch.

'Erin, I don't even know Morse code!' Sophie laughed as they struggled.

'Thank goodness!' Erin giggled.

'Hey, would anyone like one of my mum's cookies?' asked Joanna.

Together the girls spread out the blankets they'd brought with them, poured their sweets and snacks into the middle, and settled down to eat.

'I think Mark might like me a little bit, though,' Erin continued, once all the cookies were gone. 'Because when the coach stopped in Turlingham village I saw him, and he asked to borrow my comb.' She held it up proudly. 'This very comb!'

Sophie nudged Lauren. 'That definitely sounds like Mark!' Lauren covered her mouth to hide a giggle.

'I'm going to think of him every time I do my hair.' Erin kissed the comb, then exclaimed, as the others fell about laughing, 'Ooh, look – a blond hair! It's got to be his!' She held it up. 'Guys, I know: we should use his hair to cast a spell to make him fall in love with me!'

'Yeah!' said Joanna.

Sophie smiled. 'Great idea.' They'd played around with love spells before, but not for ages. *And if it helps Erin deal with her massive crush . . .* What was the harm?

Erin looked thoughtful. 'Put my scarf over the torch so it's nearly completely dark. That's for the witchy atmosphere.'

'Oh, this is a bit scary,' said Lauren, shivering as the light dimmed. A clap of thunder sounded and lightning made the windows glare. The girls shrieked and jumped, but the shrieks quickly turned into giggles.

'OK, shush now!' Erin commanded. 'This is very serious. Everyone gather round.'

The girls shuffled obediently into a circle on the blanket. Sophie squeezed between Lauren and Kaz. Erin solemnly placed the comb, with Mark's hair still glinting, in the centre of the circle.

'Close your eyes,' she told them. 'Clear your minds of all thoughts ... Now ... Hold your hands aloft—'

'*Aloft*?' There were sniggers from Kaz, echoed by Joanna. Sophie concentrated on keeping her eyes squeezed tight.

'And repeat after me this solemn spell ... Er ... '

'Hurry up then,' said Sophie. 'My hands are getting tired of being aloft.' There were more giggles from Kaz and Joanna.

'Um ... I can't think of anything to say,' Erin admitted.

'I'll do it,' said Sophie. She paused for a second before saying, 'Forces of the Earth, hear us.'

There was a sudden lull in the storm, almost as if the wind and rain were stopping to listen to her words.

'Forces of the Earth, hear us,' the girls repeated, waving their hands slowly in front of them.

'Forces of the Earth, hear us,' Sophie repeated, her voice growing quieter. The words came easily. She no longer felt like laughing. Instead, she felt calm and peaceful. Her finger tingled where the ring was touching it.

'Forces of the Earth, hear us.' The girls' voices seemed older, and stronger, and there was a strange echo in the room.

'Earth, water, wind and fire,' Sophie said slowly.

'Earth, water, wind and fire,' repeated her friends.

Sophie felt strangely alive, as if a kind of electricity was running through her. Her ring finger had pins and needles in it now. For a second she wondered if what she was saying really did have some power.

'Use your great forces to make Mark fancy Erin,' she said finally.

The ring was really glowing in the soft torchlight, the crescent moon shining like a lamp. *It must have worked its way back round*, Sophie realised. She glanced around the silent circle of her friends, their hands still raised in the air.

Can they feel it too? she wondered. *Is something really happening?*

Kaz spluttered out a giggle, and the circle broke up as the girls fell about laughing.

'Sophie, that was hilarious!' Erin laughed.

For a moment Sophie felt disappointed, and then a bit silly. But before she could get embarrassed, Kaz interrupted her thoughts.

'So, um, are you going to be seeing Callum any time soon?' she said.

'And why do you want to know?' Sophie asked with a cheeky grin. *I just let my imagination run away with me*, she thought, *that's all.*

'Oh, no reason,' Kaz replied.

'As if! Kaz, you're blushing.'

Sophie shone the torch in her friend's face, and Kaz giggled and ducked, protesting, 'I'm not *that* crazy about him!'

'Oh, well, if you don't want him, I'll have him,' Joanna said. 'So would most of the girls at Turlingham, I bet.'

'No, no, I'll have him!' Kaz said hurriedly. 'Oh, Sophie, you're so lucky to be able to see him in the holidays too. I don't know how I managed to get through six weeks without looking at his face.'

Sophie shook her head, laughing. 'I just don't get this crush on Callum!'

'You don't have to get it, you just have to spill.' Kaz sighed. 'Tell me about life as Callum's next door neighbour.'

'Well, this summer we went to the beach and the village and hung out at the ice cream shop. Thrilling stuff, huh?'

'What's his favourite flavour ice cream?' Joanna demanded, sitting up.

'Yes, give us the inside scoop!' Erin chimed in, making all the girls giggle again.

'What's he into?' asked Kaz. 'What does he like?'

'Computers,' said Sophie, rolling her eyes. 'Talk to him about computers and you can't go wrong. He likes ... pizza, and what else? Oh yes, that Roy Bears programme.'

'*Walking with Danger*?' asked Lauren.

'Yeah, that's it. But I don't think he could ever actually go on one of those wilderness camping trips – he would hate having no internet access!'

'What sort of girls does he like?' Joanna said, playing with her hair.

'I know he *doesn't* like girlie girls.' Sophie grinned. 'So you'll have to stop wearing pink if you want to impress him, Jo!'

Kaz sighed. 'I do not understand how you can be so cool around him!' A dreamy expression came over her face. 'Doesn't he make your knees go weak, and your chest go tight, and your tummy go funny—'

'Er, no!' Sophie laughed. 'Look, I've known Callum

for ever. When you've seen someone pick their nose, the magic's gone.'

There was a chorus of '*Eeew!*' and Kaz threw a wine gum at Sophie. 'So*phie*! Callum Pearce does *not* pick his nose – he's not capable of it! Now tell us how come you're immune.'

Sophie caught the wine gum, laughing back at Kaz. 'I prefer boys who are, you know . . . a bit more stylish.'

'Oh, right, this would be your Jareth Quinn obsession!' Erin said with a grin.

Sophie giggled. 'Yeah, OK, maybe I'm holding out for the best!'

Just as she spoke, the room was plunged into darkness. Lauren squealed and clutched Sophie's arm.

'The batteries have gone!' Kaz said, shaking the torch.

'I hate the dark,' Lauren said in a small voice.

Sophie could feel Lauren shivering, and wanted to make her laugh.

'That's OK,' she said, 'we'll just magic some up. Oh, Forces of the Earth, let's have some light!'

There was a split second of silence, then a clap of

40

thunder, so loud that for a moment Sophie thought the lighthouse was collapsing. At the same instant, the windows flared with lightning and the shadows of the school stood out black and white. The lighthouse shook and the windows rattled.

Everyone screamed.

There was a sizzling bang and suddenly light blazed from the giant bulb in the lantern. Sophie saw the girls' shocked faces lit up as they blinked.

'Oh my god!' shrieked Erin.

Sophie jumped up.

With a great grinding noise the ancient lighthouse's huge brass lantern began to turn. Whirling round. Working, for the first time in fifty years.

The girls screamed again and all ran for the door.

FOUR

Sophie's heart thumped wildly as she ran down the winding stairs. She jumped the last few and headed for the door. As she grabbed the handle, Lauren cried out, 'Wait! We can't go back across the courtyard, the light's shining on to it. We'll be seen!'

The girls gasped and Lauren stifled a sob.

'Don't panic,' said Sophie. 'There's another way round the courtyard. We can sneak through the trees behind Callum's house and get in through a side door. But we'll have to be quick and quiet!'

'And prepared to get wet,' Kaz said.

The girls all nodded to one another. Sophie pulled the door open with a creak and looked out. The beam from the lighthouse lamp cut through the rain as it flashed round and round. Just then a light came on in the main school building. There was no time to waste. Sophie took a deep breath and pulled her jumper up around her ears.

'Follow me!' she said, rushing out into the driving rain. Her shoes splashed in the mud as she headed for the gap in the fence, ducked through and then dived to the right. She tried to look back to see if the others were following, but she could barely make them out through the water in her eyes.

They ran along the edge of the little wood that separated Callum's garden from the lighthouse meadow. Sophie stopped when she got to the wall of the main building.

'Are we all here?' she asked, straining to see in the darkness.

'I think I've drowned,' Erin panted, wiping the rain out of her eyes. 'Where's this side door?'

'Jo – is there a bench next to you?'

Joanna, who was standing next to the wall, nodded. 'Yes.'

'Take a look. There should be a door behind it,' Sophie instructed.

Joanna felt up and down the wall. 'You're right!'

'Quick, get the bench out of the way,' Sophie told the others, and they all rushed to pull it to one side, revealing a wooden door.

'It goes into a storeroom,' said Sophie. 'We can get through into the main school building.'

Sophie pushed it open and looked into a small room that smelled strongly of dust. To either side, old desks, chairs, filing cabinets, and even an ancient slide projector, were piled up. The girls all scrambled in and Sophie shut the door behind them as they wrung out their hair and clothes.

On the other side of the storeroom was another door. Sophie made her way towards it.

'Hurry, before we get caught!' Joanna whispered behind her.

Sophie tried the handle, breathing a sigh of relief

as it turned to reveal a moonlit corridor with doors down one side and windows along the other. 'We're safe!'

'Brilliant!' Kaz exclaimed, leading the way. The others followed quickly, and Sophie went last, shutting the door behind her. They raced on tiptoes past the music practice rooms. On the walls, shadows of the trees tossed in the wind and rain. The friends slowed when they reached the end of the corridor and came out into the open space of the main entrance hall. In front of them, the wide main stairs led up into shadows; to the left were the double doors to the girls' dorms and to the right the boys' dorms.

'You're the best, Sophie,' said Kaz. 'We'd never have got out of the lighthouse without you.'

'Yeah, go Sophie!' added Erin, raising her hand for a high five. Sophie was about to slap Erin's palm when a noise from the direction of the girls' dorms wiped the smile off her face.

'Shush! I heard something,' Sophie whispered.

In the tense silence, she heard the unmistakeable

creak of a door swinging shut. The girls stared at each other.

'Hide!' Erin mouthed, lowering her hand. She scooted into the shadows, closely followed by Lauren. Kaz looked wildly left and right and dived into the shadow of a statue. Joanna ducked under a side table where copies of the school magazine were laid out for visitors.

As Sophie looked for a place to hide she caught sight of a dark figure in a large mirror on the wall opposite. As the figure turned, a well-polished prefect's badge shone on the lapel of her dressing gown. It was Maggie Millar!

Noooo! thought Sophie. Sophie knew there was a cleaning cupboard under the main stairs, so she scurried towards it. She closed herself in and winced as the door snicked shut. She could see the dim light of a torch beam at the bottom of the door and crossed her fingers, hoping Maggie hadn't heard the little noise. In the darkness, Sophie stood and listened for footsteps. The smell of cleaning products was really strong and she wrinkled her nose, trying not to sneeze.

The footsteps came closer. Then they stopped. She looked down to see torchlight shining directly on her feet, lighting up the toes of her soaking wet shoes. She placed her hand on the door handle and her heart sank even further as, very slowly, it was turning. She tried to hold it still. *Maybe she'll think it's locked and move on.* But Maggie was stronger than her, and the handle turned despite her efforts.

Please, let her not see me! Sophie thought as hard as she could. And then – even though she knew it was silly, she whispered, 'Forces of the Earth – stop her from seeing me!'

The door was yanked open and Sophie shut her eyes automatically as the torch beam flashed into them. She tensed herself for Maggie's triumphant yell . . .

A loud crash echoed through the hall. Sophie jumped.

'Who's that?' Maggie exclaimed.

Sophie opened her eyes to see Maggie looking down the hall. The door shut and she heard Maggie's footsteps running away towards the noise. She couldn't believe it, but it seemed as though Maggie hadn't seen her.

Underneath the ring, her finger suddenly flared with heat, as if she had burned it in a candle flame. She slid the ring along her finger and rubbed at the burned spot. Then she jumped again as the door was snatched open.

'Sophie!' Kaz stood there, grinning at her.

'Kaz! You scared me!' Sophie giggled in relief, stepping out of the cupboard.

'Quick, let's get back to the dorm while the coast is clear!' Lauren hissed.

'How lucky were you, Sophie?' added Erin, from behind Kaz.

'Oh, please let's get to the dorm before she comes back!' Joanna was shivering and hugging herself.

'Jo's right,' Sophie agreed. 'We'd better not push it!'

The next day at break time, Sophie slipped off to the school's gigantic library. Rows upon rows of shelves housed leather-bound books and gilt-edged encyclopaedias. Once she had found a quiet corner, she pulled the ring out of her pocket and slipped it on to a length of black ribbon that she'd got from Textiles class. She stared at the ring. It was so beautiful ... but she knew she had to put it back. The burning sensation that the ring had given her left Sophie feeling jittery. *It doesn't feel right. I shouldn't have taken it.* Twice Mrs Freeman had almost seen it, and she was really strict about confiscating jewellery. Sophie tied it around her neck, making sure it was hidden under her clothes. *It'll be safe there*, she thought. *Until I can put it back.*

As she left the library, her phone vibrated with a text from Erin.

> OMG HOT NEWS GIRLS!!! C U UNDER
> OLD OAK TREE IN 5 FOR MAJOR
> GOSSIP SESH!!!!

As Sophie was reading it, another text appeared, this one from Lauren.

> SOPHIE, WHERE R U? ERIN'S GOT
> NEWS BUT WE CAN'T START WITHOUT
> U! XX

Sophie hastily sent a reply saying she'd be there, and headed out to the courtyard. There were twigs scattered everywhere from the storm the night before, and as she walked towards her friends, she could see that a fallen branch had smashed a ground floor window – the caretaker was cordoning it off. *I bet that's what startled Maggie*, she thought.

'Oh, Sophie, please hurry up!' Lauren called as she saw her approaching. 'I can't wait to hear Erin's news!'

Sophie broke into a run. As she reached them, Erin grabbed her and squealed, 'You're not going to believe it! Mark just asked me to be his Facebook friend!'

The girls screamed in delight.

Lauren's eyes widened. 'Oh, Erin! Does that mean he's your boyfriend?'

'I think he has to ask me out first,' said Erin, laughing. 'But I'm sooo excited! And – *and*,' she bounced up and down, 'he sent me a really, really nice, I mean *really* cute message, saying, *Thank you for lending me the comb*!'

'Wow, that's brilliant!' Sophie gave her a huge hug

and Lauren joined in. 'I bet he's going to ask you on a date.'

'Ooh yes – what will you wear, if he does?' Lauren added.

Erin opened her mouth to reply, but as she glanced over Sophie's shoulder, her expression changed from excitement to astonishment.

'Check that out!' she said, pointing.

Sophie turned round, wondering what on earth could have taken Erin's mind off her news. The largest limousine she had ever seen was pulling in the wrought-iron gates at the front of the school. The girls stared in silent amazement as the sleek black car drew to a halt.

'But who does it belong to?' Lauren wondered.

'It can't be anyone at Turlingham,' said Sophie. 'Mum would have mentioned if we had millionaires in the school!'

As she watched, the driver's side opened and a smartly dressed chauffeur got out, adjusting his gold-braided cap. He opened the back door and a girl about Sophie's age emerged. She had shoulder length, perfectly styled jet black hair, and she was wearing a Turlingham uniform. The girl looked slowly around the courtyard.

'That's it!' Sophie exclaimed, turning to her friends. 'I remember now: Mum said a brother and sister were joining the school today.'

The girl brushed a strand of hair out of her eyes and moved away from the car.

'Doesn't she walk just like a model?' exclaimed Erin. 'Maybe she's someone famous.'

'I hope she's in our year,' Lauren said.

'Yeah, we totally need some new blood in Year 9,' agreed Erin. 'But she looks too grown-up. She'll be in Year 10 at least.'

'Those must be her parents,' said Joanna.

A man and a woman were getting out of the limousine. They clustered around the girl and Sophie saw them handing her a mobile phone. The woman wagged her finger as she spoke, and Sophie suddenly felt sorry for the new girl. It seemed as if her parents didn't give her much space.

'It must be scary starting a new school,' she said,

turning to her friends. 'We should make sure she feels welcome.'

'Oh, look!' Lauren interrupted her, grabbing her arm. 'That must be the brother.'

Sophie gasped. A boy was getting out of the back. He was wearing the Turlingham uniform too, he had the same black hair as the girl and he was really, really good looking.

'It's Jareth Quinn!' Erin gasped. She looked closer. 'Oh – no, it isn't.'

'He does look really like him, though,' exclaimed Lauren.

'Yeah, he does . . . Sophie!' Erin gave Sophie a teasing nudge.

Sophie quickly shut her mouth, which had fallen open in admiration, and turned to her friends.

'Do I look OK?' she demanded, quickly straightening her school tie. 'Because we, girls, are going over there to say hi to the new arrivals.'

'Oh no, Sophie,' Joanna protested. 'That's beyond embarrassing! I'm staying here. . . '

'Well, I'm the headmistress's daughter and it is

my duty to make Jareth Quinn's twin feel welcome. And you're my besties so *somebody* has to come with me!'

'I'm up for it!' Erin giggled. 'Come on, Lauren!' She hooked her arm through her friend's and they followed Sophie towards the limousine.

Sophie felt her confidence slipping away as the new arrivals stared at her. Close to, the girl and boy looked even more impressive: their uniforms fitted perfectly, as if they'd had them tailored.

'Hello, and welcome to Turlingham!' she said quickly, before she could chicken out. 'My name's Sophie. I'm Mrs Morrow's daughter. These are my friends – Erin and Lauren. It's really nice to meet you.' She fell silent. The parents were staring at her in an assessing way that made her feel uncomfortable. To make matters worse, she could see now that the mother had a nasty-looking scar all across one side of her face. It was hard not to look at it. But to her delight the boy gave her a dazzling smile and stepped forward.

'Thanks for the welcome!' he said. 'My name's Ashton, Ashton Gibson. I'm *sure* I'm going to like it here.' His green eyes sparkled at Sophie, who hoped that she wasn't blushing too much. She looked across at his sister – but the girl didn't seem to be listening. There was an awkward silence, and then the woman smiled.

'Pleased to meet you. I'm Mrs Gibson, and this is my husband.'

'Hello!' Mr Gibson said with a smile. Like his wife, Sophie noticed, he had a faint Scottish accent.

Mrs Gibson placed a hand on the girl's shoulder and said, 'Come on, Katy, aren't you going to introduce yourself?'

The girl glanced over quickly, with a flash of green eyes exactly like her brother's, and muttered a brief, 'Hi.'

'She's just shy, I'm afraid.' Mrs Gibson said this with a warm smile, and Sophie decided that the odd looks before had just been her imagination. 'It's so kind of you to welcome Ashton and Katy. We hope you'll show them around and make sure they make lots of friends as soon as possible.'

'Of course, we'd love to help.' Sophie smiled at Katy

again, but Katy looked away, playing with the mobile phone. Sophie's smile faltered.

'What year are you girls in?' Mrs Gibson asked.

'We're all in Year 9,' said Lauren.

'How lovely! So is Katy.'

'Oh cool!' Erin exclaimed. 'We were hoping you'd be in our year.'

Mrs Gibson beamed.

'There, isn't that nice, Katy? You've met your class-mates already.'

Katy muttered something inaudible and glanced sideways at Erin. Her pretty jade earrings caught sparks in the light as she moved.

'Katy …' said Mrs Gibson, sounding annoyed. 'She's feeling a bit nervous,' she added to Sophie. Sophie forced a smile, not knowing what to say. Ashton caught her eye and gave her a gorgeous grin.

'*I'm* in Year 10,' he said. 'But I'm sure we'll see plenty of each other.'

Sophie felt her heart speed up. To her relief, Lauren broke the moment, piping up: 'That's a lot of luggage!'

The chauffer had unloaded a stack of monogrammed trunks.

'We'll help carry it,' offered Sophie, reaching for Katy's suitcase. But to her astonishment, Katy suddenly lunged across and pulled the suitcase out of her way.

'I'm sorry!' Katy blurted out. 'It's just – I'd better carry it.' She pulled it protectively towards her.

'Er – OK,' Sophie said, trying not to show her surprise.

'It's heavy. I wouldn't want you to hurt yourself,' Katy said, ducking her head again so her hair shielded her face.

'Oh, I think Sophie can take care of herself,' drawled Ashton. He removed a pair of sunglasses from his blazer pocket and put them on – but not before he'd given Sophie a wink. Sophie tried to stop herself from grinning ear to ear, and exchanged a delighted glance with Erin. Erin's raised eyebrow said clearly: *I think you've got a fan!*

'It's very kind of you, but James can manage the bags.' Mr Gibson nodded towards the chauffeur, who was already carrying the trunks. 'Now, can you tell me where the head teachers' offices are?'

Sophie explained how to get there, and the four Gibsons headed off towards the main entrance.

'Thank you again for your help,' the mother purred. 'It won't be forgotten.' Sophie watched until the door shut behind them, and then spun towards her friends.

'How cute was he? He *winked* at me!'

'I know! Oh my god, I'm sure he was flirting!' Erin responded. 'But the girl's weird – I mean, she couldn't even say hello? How rude!'

'Maybe she's just really shy like her mum said,' suggested Sophie.

'Or really stuck up,' said Kaz.

Sophie shrugged. 'We ought to give her a chance ... Anyone with a brother that hot can't be all bad!'

FIVE

Sophie had been looking forward to daydreaming about Ashton in the History lesson that followed. But all she could think about was the ring. She could feel it resting against her skin, cold and uncomfortably scratchy. At least it wasn't burning any more.

OK, that's it, she thought. *I'm going to put it back right now.*

She raised her hand. Mr McGowan pounced. 'Yes, Sophie, you have a question?'

'Sorry, Mr McGowan, I just wanted to go to the bathroom.'

Mr McGowan sighed and nodded. As she went out of the door she heard him continue, '*Someone* must be inspired by the fifteenth-century woollen industry – come on, don't any of you have a question?'

Sophie headed down the corridor, but instead of going into the girls' toilets she continued to her mother's office. At the door, she glanced around to check the coast was clear, then put her ear to the wood. She'd been hoping the office would be empty, but to her disappointment she heard the rumble of voices. She was about to step away when she heard a name that made her turn back: 'Ashton ... ' She hesitated. She didn't exactly mean to listen in, but the people inside seemed to be talking very loudly – or else, she thought, her hearing was surprisingly good today.

'The school is lovely, Mrs Morrow.' Sophie recognised Mrs Gibson's faint Scottish accent.

'I'm glad you like it.' Her mother didn't sound overjoyed, though. 'But I have just one question. I notice that Katy and Ashton have, between them, been to seven schools in the last two years. Why is this?'

Sophie's eyes widened. Seven schools in two years! But she heard Mr and Mrs Gibson laughing.

'Nothing sinister, I can assure you!' Mr Gibson exclaimed. 'It's not ideal, but, you see, my job demands so much travel and we prefer to keep the children with us as much as possible.'

'I see.' Mrs Morrow didn't sound convinced. 'Because no doubt you understand such disruption can be hard to deal with . . . '

Remembering that she was eavesdropping, Sophie stepped away from the door. She turned and headed back to class. *I'll put the ring back later*, she promised herself. *As soon as I possibly can.*

'Sophie, are you going to eat that baked potato or just stare at Ashton Gibson?' Erin demanded with a cheeky grin.

Sophie blushed and hastily took a mouthful. 'I'm not staring – I was just daydreaming.'

'Yeah, and we know who you're daydreaming

63

about! Can't blame you – he totally looks like Jareth Quinn. No wonder you're swooning,' Kaz teased, doing a mock faint into Joanna's arms.

'I'm not!' Sophie laughed. 'Hey, look,' she added, to distract her friends, 'there's his sister.'

The girls watched as Katy edged through the lunch hall, carrying her tray. She made eye contact with no one and ignored the few stares she got. When she glanced in their direction Sophie smiled at her, but Katy made for an empty table by the open window. She sat down, pulled out her phone and began to tap away at the keys, now and then looking up and surveying the room.

'Well, that's not very friendly,' exclaimed Kaz.

Sophie hesitated, remembering: *seven schools in two years*. She was sure that if her friends knew that, they wouldn't be so hard on Katy. But it wasn't her secret to tell, so she just said, 'It must be difficult being the only new girl.'

'Hmm, I don't know,' Joanna said. 'Look how she's staring at everyone. As if she doesn't think we're good enough for her.' The others murmured in agreement.

'Well, I think she looks lonely over there on her own,' said Sophie. 'I'm going to ask her to come and sit with us.'

She stood up and made her way across the room. Katy slid her phone into her pocket.

'Katy, you don't have to sit alone,' Sophie said with a smile as she reached her. 'You could join our table.'

Katy blushed.

'But if you *do* want to sit on your own,' Sophie continued, 'don't sit here. There's a reason this table is empty: the lovely stink from the rubbish bins outside.'

Katy's cold expression wavered, and she laughed. Sophie grinned, glad that she had a sense of humour.

'Come on.' She nodded over at the table where her friends were sitting. 'We don't bite – honestly.'

Katy hesitated, then smiled. 'Yeah, OK. Thanks.'

As they reached the table, Sophie pointed to each of her friends. 'This is Kaz, Joanna, Lauren and—'

'And I'm Erin!' Erin jumped up and pulled out a chair. Katy slid into the seat, crossing her arms. As soon as she sat down, the girls started talking.

'I love your perfume!' said Kaz.

'What do you think of the school?' asked Lauren.

'What dorm are you in?' asked Joanna.

'I noticed you were texting like crazy over there. Chatting to your boyfriend?' Erin asked with a grin.

Katy sighed. 'I wish,' she admitted. 'Just my parents – boring, I know.'

Sophie knew she was lucky not to have to feel homesick – the school *was* her home. But before she could think of something comforting to say, a hand grasped her shoulder. Sophie yelped and turned round.

'Uh ... Maggie! Hi.'

Maggie leaned in, her prefect badge flashing in the light.

'Funny the things that happen in this school,' she said, staring hard at each of the girls in turn. 'Take the lighthouse, for example. Out of bounds, as you no doubt know. And yet ... ' her eyes snapped to Sophie's face, 'someone turned the beacon on last night.'

Sophie glanced at her friends, who were sitting with frozen expressions.

'Um, did they?' she said, her voice wobbling slightly.

Maggie nodded slowly.

'Yes indeed. And *someone* left wet footprints all the way down the hall. I've made a note of it in my Unsolved Crimes file. But it won't be unsolved for long. I know who did it, you see.'

'W-who?' Sophie quavered.

'Don't try that innocent act with me!' Maggie snapped. She tapped her badge. 'You don't get made Head Prefect for nothing. I've used my brains, and I'm sure it was you five.'

Sophie gulped, but Kaz spoke up.

'It wasn't us, Maggie. We don't know what you mean, do we?' She glanced around, and the others shook their heads innocently as they caught on.

'I saw five silhouettes against the light – and I know which gang of five is always making trouble around here! Simple deduction. And besides – I found this in the hall the next morning.' She whisked something out of her pocket. It was Erin's scarf.

'That's not proof,' said Sophie quickly. 'Erin could have dropped it any time.'

'Yeah!' Erin smiled brightly as she plucked the scarf

out of Maggie's hand and draped it round her neck. 'In fact, I remember I lost it yesterday just after I arrived. Thanks for finding it, Maggie. I owe you one.'

Sophie stifled a nervous giggle at the expression on Maggie's face.

'Fine,' snapped Maggie. 'Maybe I can't prove it – but if I catch you up there again, I'm telling the teachers. As the Head Prefect it's my duty to report irresponsible and dangerous behaviour.' She gave them an evil look and stalked off.

Sophie massaged her shoulder where Maggie had grabbed it. The girls sat in silence. The cheerful mood was gone.

Finally Katy whispered, 'So what was that about?'

There was an awkward silence, then Lauren said quickly, 'Oh, we have midnight parties sometimes. We had a brilliant one last night. We went up into the old lighthouse,' she lowered her voice as she spoke, 'and the light just came on of its own accord when we were up there! It hasn't worked for fifty years!'

'Dude, that was so scary!' Erin exclaimed. 'I just don't get how it came on like that! Totally ghostly!'

'Maybe it was the magic spell,' Kaz said with a laugh. Sophie laughed with everyone else, but Katy looked at Kaz with sudden interest.

'Midnight parties sound fun,' she said, leaning forwards. 'What sort of things do you do?'

Kaz shrugged. 'Oh, we just have fun and mess around. Last night Erin had the idea to cast a love spell on Mark.'

Katy raised her eyebrows. 'Really?'

'He's the one over on the other side of the hall, with the spiky blond hair,' said Joanna, pointing him out.

'Nice choice, Erin,' Katy said with a smile that made Erin blush. She suddenly seemed much more animated. 'So, did it work?'

'Um, yeah, actually, it did!' Erin said, as the others nodded. 'He even sent me a message this morning – look.' She held out her phone to Katy, who put her own down on the table and read it with a smile.

'He sounds keen!' Katy remarked as she studied the text. 'I'll have to teach you the boy-snaring tactics I learned at my last school.'

'Awesome,' breathed Erin.

Katy smiled, and her green eyes flashed as she handed Erin back her phone. 'Maybe we could have another party tonight? I've got lots of ideas for games to make it extra spooky.'

'Brilliant!' Kaz exclaimed.

Joanna nodded enthusiastically but added, 'We can't go to the lighthouse again if Maggie's watching for us.'

'What about having it in the storeroom Sophie showed us?' suggested Lauren. 'She won't think of looking for us there.'

'Yeah! That would work,' Erin agreed.

She caught Sophie's eye and smiled widely. Sophie smiled back – but she wondered why she wasn't feeling happier. After all, it seemed like Katy was nice. But there was going to be another midnight party that night and she wouldn't be able to go because she'd be back at home! She felt the smile slide off her face. She *had* to go!

Sophie couldn't help feeling worried. It looked as if being good was not going to be possible this term at all!

SIX

Sophie checked her phone as she hurried down the path. 11.45 p.m. – perfect timing. She glanced back at the house, half expecting her mother to come running after her. But there was no light from the cottage; in fact she almost thought she could still hear her mum's quiet, regular breathing as she slept. She'd paused outside her mum's bedroom doorway, listening at the crack in the door to the sound of her mum sleeping, before letting herself out of the cottage.

Sophie breathed a sigh of relief as she vaulted over the low fence that surrounded her garden. Keeping to the shadows, she headed towards the storeroom, texting Erin and Lauren as she went.

I'M ON MY WAY!

She listened for the beep of an answering text as she walked, but it didn't come. That was odd – they usually texted back in seconds. *I hope nothing's stopped them getting to the storeroom,* she thought as she got closer. She rounded the corner – and stopped dead.

In front of her was a bench outside the sick bay that the girls sometimes sat on at break times. A bird was perched on one of the arm rests. Could it be the same raven she'd seen the night before? The raven cocked its head in her direction and ruffled its feathers.

Sophie took a step back.

'Are you following me or something?' she said aloud. She wondered why she felt so uneasy. It was just a bird, after all.

The bird wasn't alone. As her eyes got used to

the shadows, she made out a squirrel sitting on the bench next to it. The two animals stared at her, not in fear, more as if she had interrupted an important conversation. Sophie almost felt like apologising. She shook her head. As if they could even understand her!

'Shoo!' she said instead, flapping at them. The squirrel and the raven looked at each other, and then at her. Neither of them made a move.

Sophie opened her mouth to try again, but before she could speak the raven flapped its wings and let out a sharp *craw*. The squirrel scampered off the bench and disappeared in the shadows. Then the raven took flight, its glossy wings flapping away over the cliffs.

Sophie couldn't see what had startled the animals, but better safe than sorry. She flattened herself against the wall of the sick bay, hiding in the darkness.

A second later, the back door opened and a thin figure stepped out. Sophie's eyes widened as it came into the moonlight. It was Mrs Freeman.

Mrs Freeman looked left and right, frowning.

'I thought I heard something out here,' she said to

someone still inside the building. 'I must have been mistaken.'

Sophie let out a silent sigh of relief as Mrs Freeman retreated. She waited until she had heard the lock being fastened before coming out from her hiding place and tiptoeing across the courtyard, as fast as she could towards the storeroom. As she moved, a single thought pulsed through her.

Erin and Lauren *still* hadn't texted back. Where were they?

Sophie edged along the wall. She could see a dull square of light ahead of her. It was a tiny window, next to the storeroom door. She stood on tiptoe and peered through it.

Through the dusty glass, she could see into the storeroom. It was lit by a flickering, eerie light that came from four candles of black wax in silver holders. Five figures were crouched around a wooden board that was decorated with letters and numbers. It was her friends and Katy. Sophie was startled to find she could hear their voices even through the glass.

'Katy, this is amazing,' Erin was saying, as she leaned over the board.

'Yeah, where did you find these candles?' Kaz asked.

Sophie pulled back, feeling a little hurt. So that was why they hadn't answered her texts – they were just having too much fun with Katy to bother. They hadn't even thought to wait for her. But she quickly reproached herself for being mean. Erin and Lauren weren't going to drop her just because a new girl turned up with some black candles!

There was a sudden crunch, so loud it sounded as if someone was eating crisps next to her. Sophie gasped and spun round. In a second, she spotted torchlight wavering across the courtyard and realised the noise had been footsteps on gravel. Someone was walking towards her, sweeping their torch from left to right like a searchlight.

Sophie flattened herself back into the shadows under the window. Her heart beat fast as she peered along the wall to see who it was. The person paused to zip up her coat and the moonlight fell on to her face.

Sophie caught her breath. It was Maggie Millar again. Was that girl stalking them?

Sophie's mind worked fast as Maggie began her patrol once more. In just a few moments she would see Sophie, and then she'd see the light from the window – and her friends would be caught. Sophie had to warn them.

She thrust open the door a couple of inches and hissed, 'Maggie's coming! Hide!'

She didn't wait to see if they'd understood. There was no time. She ran, kicking up the gravel to make as much noise as she could, across the courtyard. She had to draw Maggie's attention away from the others. She heard Maggie exclaim and the torchlight bobbed after her. Knowing she needed to lead her as far away as possible, Sophie slowed down and pretended not to hear her footsteps pounding up. Maggie's hand closed on her arm and Sophie whipped round, gasping in pretend surprise but secretly delighted that she had saved her friends.

'Now you've done it!' Maggie laughed triumphantly, shining the torch into her face. 'I don't know what you're smirking about,' she added. 'You might be the headmistress's daughter, but you can't get out of this heap of trouble!'

'I can't believe this of you, Sophie! I am so very, very disappointed.'

Sophie stared at the carpet. She felt close to tears. Her mother paced back and forth behind her office desk, her arms folded over her dressing gown. Maggie stood smugly by the door, blocking the exit.

'After I allowed you to stay in the dorms the other night, too. Really, I'm shocked. Haven't you any expla-nation for this behaviour?'

Sophie shook her head silently. She didn't want to lie, and the truth would only get her friends into trouble.

'It's dangerous to run around outside at night,' Maggie piped up, one eye on Mrs Morrow. 'As all the girls should know from their inductions—'

'Yes, Maggie, thank you,' said Mrs Morrow hastily. She turned back to Sophie. 'As your mother, Sophie, I'm grounding you. But as your head teacher . . . ' Her eyes went to Maggie. 'On second thoughts, I think it would be better if Maggie decided your punishment. After all, you've put her to great inconvenience too.'

'Oh, I don't mind at all, Mrs Morrow,' Maggie said quickly. 'A Head Prefect has certain responsibilities. As for a punishment . . . ' She paused and Sophie held her breath. 'How about, let's say, extra prep for a week?'

'That's very fair, Maggie.' Mrs Morrow nodded. 'And Sophie, you can use your break times, when you might have been with your friends, to do that extra prep.' She stifled a yawn. 'Now, I think we all need our sleep. Good night, Maggie – and thank you.'

Sophie followed her mother back to their cottage in gloomy silence. She knew how angry she'd made her and she wished she could explain. It looked as if there'd be no more sneaking out to join midnight feasts, and, now that she was grounded, she wouldn't be able to see her friends in break time either. She'd been so looking forward to the start of term – but it was turning out to be disastrous! She slipped a hand inside the collar of her hoodie to feel the ring that still hung from the black velvet. She still hadn't managed to put it back in her mum's office drawer. *How did I get in such a mess so early in the year?* she wondered.

At least she'd managed to save her friends from being discovered. But, for now, sneaking about had stopped being fun.

As Sophie pushed open the door of her classroom the next morning she noticed something different about the familiar uproar. As usual, groups of friends were sitting on desks, joking and chatting and gossiping before the teacher came to take the register. But today, each conversation seemed to be about one thing: *Katy!*

'I love Katy's hair!' she heard one girl saying to another as she went down the rows of desks. 'Have you seen how she does it, with that side parting? I'm going to try mine like that.'

'She has such cool music on her iPod!'

'Did you see Katy's pyjamas? I'm going to ask my mum to buy me some!'

Looks like she's made a good impression, thought Sophie. She could see Katy sitting at the back of the classroom surrounded by Erin, Lauren, Kaz and Jo. She lifted her hand to wave, but Katy was talking animatedly, and no one looked her way. As she reached them, the group burst into peals of laughter.

'Oh, Katy, you are sooo funny!' Erin wiped tears from her eyes.

Sophie smiled too, though she hadn't a clue what the joke was. She sat down behind them at a spare desk, realising as she did so that Katy was in *her* usual seat, next to Erin.

'Hey, what's so funny?' she asked.

'Oh, you had to be there,' Erin said. 'Come on, Katy, tell us more.'

'Yeah – and don't forget the penguin hat!' Lauren exclaimed, and the group burst into laughter once again.

Sophie glanced round at her friends, hoping someone would explain. But no one did. For a moment, she wished she was hanging out with Callum instead, but she knew he'd be on a computer somewhere. Callum spent all his lunch breaks on a computer or a laptop or a handheld game.

'Erin,' she began, 'you didn't text this morning? I was worried—'

'Didn't I? Oh, I was chatting to Katy.' Erin shrugged. 'And then we were all in such a rush for breakfast and, well, you know – sorry.'

Sophie opened her mouth and closed it again. Erin always texted her as soon as she got up. And not just when she got up – as she got dressed, when she was out of the bathroom ... She'd even texted from America! As the others chattered away to Katy, she was horrified to realise she was on the brink of tears.

'Erin! It's just—' She swallowed and got a hold of herself. 'I wanted to tell you, you know you were all having that party last night in the storeroom? Well, I—'

'Oh, it was amazing!' Jo burst out. 'Katy made it so much fun!'

'I didn't do anything much really.' Katy laughed and tossed her dark hair. 'I mean, apart from bring the Ouija board and the candles.'

'And the penguin hat!' Jo spluttered. The girls burst into fits of giggles again.

'But you don't realise,' said Sophie, 'Maggie—'

'Yes, Maggie nearly caught us!' Lauren said, wide-eyed.

'I know, I—'

'Someone whispered in at the door that she was coming. Oh my god, it was so scary, wasn't it?' Erin went on, looking at Katy as she spoke. 'We thought it was an actual ghost at first.'

'Well, it wasn't, it was me!' Sophie almost shouted.

'Oh!' Erin turned to her. 'Oh ... of course, that makes sense. Thanks, Sophie!' She turned back to Katy. 'Honestly, we were in such a panic, weren't we?'

'Yeah, but Katy managed to hide everything and then sneak us out,' Joanna added. 'Thanks, Katy! Oh, and Sophie, too.'

Katy's phone bleeped and she pulled it out of her bag.

'I so love your phone charms,' sighed Lauren, leaning over to admire them. A tiny set of love birds and a miniature jewellery box dangled on strands of glistening silk.

'Who's the text from, Katy?' Erin said, putting an

arm round her shoulders. The others leaned in to see.

Sophie stared at the backs of their heads in disbelief. But before she could think of anything to say, Mrs Layton, their form tutor, hurried in with the register.

Her chance to explain to her friends what she'd done to save their skins was gone. She hadn't even been able to tell them she was grounded.

SEVEN

The sports hall echoed to the thud of volleyballs and basketballs, and the occasional shriek of Mrs Butters' whistle as she jogged up and down supervising both groups at once. Sophie bounced on her toes as she waited for the volleyball to head her way.

Next to her, Anna, one of the sporty girls in Year 9, frowned.

'I can't believe how many people are trying out for the team! Volleyball is never this popular.'

Sophie was glad when Anna dived for the ball and she didn't have to answer. The reason for the crowded sports hall was in front of her, her black hair swinging as she jumped: Katy Gibson. Ever since she'd spent a stolen evening with Sophie's friends, Katy had become Miss Popularity, the person all Sophie's classmates wanted to be close to. As soon as her name had appeared on the sign-up list for volleyball, pretty much every Year 9's had magically followed it. Sophie didn't particularly like volleyball, but what with extra prep and being grounded, she felt as if she had to take every chance to be with her friends ... before they forgot about her completely!

On the other side of the hall, a group of boys including Callum, Mark Little and their friend Oliver Campbell were practising basketball. Sophie raised her hand in a wave. Callum waved back.

'Who's the geek?' Katy, pink-cheeked and breathless from running, flicked her hair out of her eyes and frowned at Callum. Sophie felt her face grow hot. Katy's shyness seemed to have melted away.

'Callum's my friend,' she said. She moved away from Katy pointedly.

'Sorry,' Katy retorted. 'I didn't know.' She headed over to the other side of the net.

'Get into teams, girls!' Mrs Butters shouted. 'Practice is over, time for a real game.'

Sophie was about to obey, but at that moment Ashton Gibson came out of the boys' changing rooms, carrying a basketball. He strolled over to the other boys, casually bouncing it as he went. Approaching the net, he broke into a run, leapt for the hoop and slam-dunked the ball through it. Sophie's jaw dropped. As he landed, he caught Sophie's eye. Sophie went bright red. But instead of laughing at her goofy expression, Ashton gave her a dreamy smile. Sophie's knees went so weak that she almost fell over. Ashton looked better than ever – even wearing the Turlingham boys' awful gym kit.

Quick, do something cool! she thought. She looked around for inspiration just as Mrs Butters blew her whistle and tossed the ball to Katy. Katy caught it and looked at Sophie. The next second the ball was shooting towards her. Taken off-guard, Sophie didn't have a chance to react. The ball thumped hard into her stomach.

'Oof!' Sophie gasped, doubling over.

'Sophie, are you OK?' Mrs Butters called over. 'Katy, be more careful.'

'Sorry,' Katy called back.

Sophie straightened up, blinking back tears of pain and embarrassment. Some of the boys were laughing and pointing at her.

She did that on purpose! Sophie thought furiously. *Right. I'll show her.* She raised the volleyball and sent it right back at Katy, who dodged. Kaz dived for it and sent the ball back on to Sophie's side of the net. The ball flew back and forth to encouraging shouts from both teams.

'You're neck and neck!' Mrs Butters called after several minutes had passed. 'Come on, girls! The next point you score wins the game.'

Sophie caught the ball as Anna tossed it to her, ready for her next serve. She scanned the other side of the court for gaps in their defence. Katy was near the net, with Erin and Kaz right behind her. She sent the ball flying into what she thought was an unguarded spot, but Katy reached it with ease and sent the ball back at her. Sophie had to lunge across the court for it. Her team yelled encouragement; she just managed to clip the ball with her hand and it shot over the net. Her ring, on its chain, thumped against her chest as she fell to the ground. The ball cleared the net, but she could see it was going to go out and lose them the game. Erin and Katy already had their hands up for a high-five. Sophie closed her eyes. All she had left now was her lucky motto.

'Forces of the Earth,' she gasped under her breath, 'keep it in!'

The ring felt suddenly hot against her skin. Her whole body tingled, as if a wave of energy were rushing through it. With a bang the doors of the sports hall blew open and a gust of wind surged in. The volleyball curved in mid-air, as if pushed by the wind, and fell to the ground – inside the baseline.

'I don't believe it!' Anna yelled. 'We win! Go, Sophie!'

Sophie, bewildered but delighted, found herself mobbed by her thrilled teammates. As she laughed and exchanged congratulations, she saw Katy on the other side of the net, walking away. A pang of guilt struck her. Of course Katy hadn't meant to hit her with the ball. Why would she do that? She broke away from her team and ran to catch up with her.

'Hey,' she said, brushing her sweaty hair out of her face, 'good game! Shake hands?' She held hers out with a smile.

Katy looked down. She seemed to hesitate, but then smiled back and shook Sophie's hand.

'Congratulations,' she said, turning away to the changing room. Sophie watched her go, half puzzled. Katy's smile hadn't seemed very sincere at all.

Sophie gazed blankly at the tangled jungle of equations in her Maths prep book and heaved a sigh. Outside, in the courtyard, she could hear the shrieks and laughter of her friends having fun. And she was stuck in a classroom, with Maggie Millar ... for the third break that week.

'You know, this is for your own good, Sophie,' Maggie told her as she put a stack of Maths textbooks down in front of her. 'You'll thank me for it one day. Rules are made to be kept, not broken. Important life lesson.'

Sophie didn't reply. She knew it wouldn't help. She bent her head over her Maths book and tried to shut out Maggie's nagging.

'... and I expect you to have finished all your prep by the time I get back.'

Sophie glanced up. Maggie was leaving the room, carrying a stack of papers for photocopying.

As the door closed behind her, Sophie stared at the pile of homework. For a second she thought about starting on it – but as soon as she looked at the first page she tossed it down in despair. Instead she went over to the window and looked out. Several people were in the courtyard. Through the jasmine that framed the window and climbed the walls of the school she saw something moving. It was a black squirrel. It stared up at her with bright, beady eyes.

But the noise of a car door slamming made her glance over to her cottage, just in time to see her mother's car pulling out of the school grounds.

Sophie's hand went to the ring around her neck.

Now's my chance to put it back! she thought. She winced as she imagined the trouble she'd be in if Maggie came back and saw she wasn't here. Then she imagined her mother's reaction if she happened to look in her drawer and find the ring was missing. Upsetting her mother was worse than upsetting Maggie, she decided.

Her mind made up, she went to the door, and, after a careful glance up and down the corridor, slipped out of the classroom. It was now or never. *I have to put the ring back where I found it*, she told herself as she hurried down the corridor.

Inside her mother's office, Sophie went straight to the desk and took the ring from around her neck. She weighed it in her hand.

It's only a ring, she told herself, pulling the drawer open.

The package was apparently undisturbed since the

last time she had touched it. As she lifted it out of the drawer, some other papers fell on to the floor. Sophie bent to pick them up – and froze in disbelief. She was looking at an envelope and, just like the package, it was addressed to her.

Sophie placed the envelope side by side with the package. The spiky, firm handwriting was the same on both labels.

Sophie's breath came fast and shallow. She turned back to the drawer and rifled through the contents. It took her just a few seconds to realise the desk was stuffed with letters, envelope after envelope – and every single one was addressed to her. A quick glance at the handwriting told her they were all from the same person.

Sophie's hands shook as she ripped an envelope open. The bell for the next lesson rang, but she ignored it. This was more important. Why had her mother kept these from her? She read the first line of the letter inside:

Sophie, I am your grandmother and I love you.

She read it over and over again. Then the ring *wasn't* from her father. It couldn't be from her mother's mother either – Granny Morrow's elegant, old-fashioned handwriting was nothing like this. It had to be from her father's mother. The woman Sophie had never met.

Tears stabbed at her eyes and the room seemed to swirl around her. She'd forgotten all about being grounded and the danger of being caught yet again. That wasn't important now. Somewhere, there was a grandmother who wanted to know her – who had been sending her letters telling her she loved her. But her own mother had stuffed them in a drawer and not even told her about them.

How could she do this to me?

'Sophie?'

Her head jerked up. Sophie's mother was standing at the office door.

EIGHT

'What on earth are you doing?'

Sophie's mum came into the office and shut the door.

'Why aren't you doing your prep?'

'I – I –' Sophie stammered.

'I can't believe this! After Maggie gave up her break to supervise you.' Her mother put her hands on her hips. 'Sophie, this is not just naughty, it's inconsiderate and selfish.'

Sophie opened her mouth to protest, but her mother

continued: 'I don't understand what's got into you lately.' She shook her head. 'Your behaviour has been terrible!'

Sophie finally found her voice.

'What about *your* behaviour?' she blurted out.

Her mother looked astonished.

'Sophie! Don't—'

Sophie cut her off. 'I found them!' She waved an envelope at her mother, who looked even more confused and angry.

'*What* did you find?'

'The letters!'

'What letters?'

Sophie delved her hand into the drawer and threw the rest of the envelopes across the desk. One fluttered to her mother's feet. Sophie's mum bent and picked it up. Her expression changed as she looked at the ancient yellow paper, brittle with age.

'Oh,' she said.

'Why did you hide them from me?' Sophie cried. 'Why didn't you tell me about my grandmother?'

'Sophie,' her mother said gently, placing the letter on the desk. 'It's not what you think—'

Sophie held up the ring, her hand shaking. 'I found this, too! She sent me a present and you never ... you didn't even ...' She burst into tears.

'Oh, Sophie!'

Her mother rushed to hug her. Sophie felt warm arms around her and sobbed.

'Sophie, Sophie.' Her mother stroked her hair. 'I'm so sorry. I'm so very sorry. I meant it for the best.'

'How could this be for the best?' Sophie demanded through her tears. 'I know you're angry with Dad for leaving. So am I. But that's not my grandmother's fault!'

Mrs Morrow shook her head. 'You don't understand.' Sophie was startled to see tears sparkling in her eyes. 'This isn't about your father. Of course it's all been very ... very difficult ... very painful... but that's not why I kept your grandmother's letters from you.' She dabbed at her eyes and said quietly, 'Have you read it properly?'

Sophie looked back at the letter.

Sophie, I am your grandmother and I love you.
I have to warn you of something: witches are real!

Sophie stared at the words. Was this a joke?

'Now look at the other letters,' Mrs Morrow said sadly.

Sophie pulled out the second letter and read the first lines:

Sophie, I am your grandmother and I love you.
I have to warn you of something: witches are real!

She pulled more envelopes from the drawer and ripped them open. The same words leapt to her eyes: *Sophie, I am your grandmother and I love you ... I have to warn you of something: witches are real ... witches are real ... witches are real ... I have to warn you ... witches are real!*

Sophie looked back up at her mother. '*Witches are real?*' she said with a frown. 'What is she talking about?'

Sophie's mother looked her in the eye. 'Your grandmother is very ill,' she said softly. 'She's in an institution. They look after her well, but she has paranoid delusions. About ... witches, for some reason.'

Sophie turned over the envelope she was holding.

The return address was on the back: the Bowden Psychiatric Hospital.

'I was going to tell you when you were older,' she said.

Sophie nodded slowly. It was hard to know what to think. Her grandmother cared about her. That was a good feeling, and she was still angry with her mother for keeping them apart. But she thought witches existed, and that was . . . well, weird, and scary.

'I did what I thought was best, Sophie, and I'm sorry I hurt you.'

'I'm sorry, too.' Sophie reached up and gave her a hug. Her mother hugged her back and looked down at the ring Sophie was still clutching.

'You can keep that, if you like,' she said. 'It's pretty, isn't it? And it is yours, after all.' She straightened up, as if a thought had just struck her. 'But do remember the rule about no jewellery with school uniform.'

Sophie giggled as her mother's tone switched back to headmistress mode.

'Yes, Mrs Morrow.'

Suddenly there was a hammering at the door. Sophie jumped and her mum turned round, startled.

She opened the door and Sophie saw Maggie Millar standing outside.

'Mrs Morrow, Mrs Morrow, she's gone!' Maggie began, her voice squeaking in indignation. 'She's – oh – *there* you are!'

Sophie tensed. This was going to be a major trouble situation.

'Maggie, Sophie must be let off her detention now,' Sophie's mum said.

'But . . . but . . .'

'There's been a family issue. I'm sorry that you've been inconvenienced, but right now Sophie needs to be at home.' She turned back to Sophie and stretched out her arms. Sophie went to her, but, as they hugged, she caught sight of Maggie's angry face behind her mother's back.

I'm watching you, Maggie mouthed, before turning and striding away down the corridor.

'Mmm, that was gorgeous, Mr Pearce, thanks!' Sophie said as she got up to help Callum clear the table.

'Yes, thanks for inviting us round for dinner,' said

Sophie's mum as she joined them in stacking plates. 'It's great to get a good meal once in a while!'

'You're welcome – it's a pleasure to have you. By the way,' Mr Pearce added as they carried the dishes through into the kitchen, 'have you had any more thoughts about the Welcome Back Dance?'

Sophie exchanged a delighted look with Callum.

'I think it would be a good idea. The pupils need to let off some steam,' Mrs Morrow answered.

'How about in two weeks' time?'

'Seriously, Mr Pearce?' exclaimed Sophie. 'A dance would be so cool.'

'Hmm, well, we've not quite made our minds up yet,' said Mrs Morrow, teasingly flicking a tea towel at her. 'But you know what might help influence our decision . . .?'

Sophie mock-groaned and caught the tea towel. 'Washing up?'

'Smart girl.'

'Come on then, Callum,' said Sophie, rolling up her sleeves. Callum sighed but followed her to the kitchen and started running water into the sink. Their parents went back into the sitting room, still discussing the dance. It was nice to be with Callum for an evening, and to be back on better terms with her mum. All the worries about her friendships and her grandmother started to melt away.

'So,' said Sophie as she dried a plate, 'have you heard anything from Mark? You know, about Erin?'

'Huh? Why would Mark be talking about Erin?' Callum frowned, looking puzzled.

'Oh, come on, Cal! You know Erin's into him. Does he fancy her?'

Callum stopped washing up and hitched his glasses up his nose, leaving a trace of soap suds.

'Hmm. I haven't heard him mention her recently. Though there is a rumour that on the first night of term he talked about her in his sleep.'

'*Really*? That's so cute!'

'Yeah, Ollie told me that he sat up in bed and shouted, "I want to ask out Erin Best." And then the lighthouse light came on. I remember that woke me up, it was so bright!'

'No way,' said Sophie thoughtfully. 'That's so strange,

because . . . ' She tailed off, deciding not to say anything about the pretend spell they had cast that night. Callum might think it was silly. 'I really hope he hasn't stopped fancying her,' she said instead. 'She really likes him.'

'Yeah, I dunno.' Callum shrugged.

'And what about the other Year 10 boys?'

'What do you mean?'

'I mean, I was just wondering, if, say, Ashton Gibson was into anyone at the moment?'

Callum's face cracked into a huge grin. 'Oh, and I wonder why you were wondering that, huh? I mean, he only looks just like Jareth Quinn. Whose posters you have all over your wall.' He ducked, laughing, as Sophie threw the tea towel at him. The towel flopped to the ground next to the door into the sitting room. Sophie ran over to pick it up and, as she bent down, she heard Mr Pearce say, 'Ashton Gibson, on the other hand . . . '

She quickly raised a hand to shush Callum.

'Listen, they're talking about him!' she whispered.

Callum gave her an odd look. 'You've got good hearing.'

'Shush – listen!'

She heard her mother respond: 'The Gibsons? Yes, I agree. There is certainly something a bit unusual about them ...'

NINE

'Take Katy, for example,' Sophie's mum continued. 'She's perfectly well behaved in class, but her work is a different matter. She just doesn't try. She doesn't seem to care.'

Sophie, her ear pressed against the kitchen door, raised her eyebrows at Callum.

'Very odd,' said Mr Pearce.

'Yes, and she has been skipping classes. She seems surgically attached to that phone of hers—'

'Ashton is exactly the same,' Mr Pearce cut in.

'She's had it confiscated four times. So I rang her parents to talk to them about it.'

'And were they concerned?'

'Hardly! They actually insisted that she should be able to use her mobile whenever she wants.'

Sophie steered Callum away from the door.

'I knew there was something weird about Katy Gibson!' she said as soon as they were out of earshot. 'I'm going to try and find out what's going on.' She hesitated. 'Why don't you keep an eye on Ashton at the same time? We could compare notes.'

Callum laughed and shook his head.

'You just want to know about Ashton because you fancy him. I'm not going to trail around after him all day just to bring you notes.'

'No, no, it's not like that,' Sophie insisted, even though she knew she was blushing. Callum folded his arms and grinned. 'Oh, all right, maybe it is!'

'I knew it! Sophie's in lurve . . . ' Callum teased.

'Callum!' Sophie laughed, her face bright red. 'But listen, you see him all day, every day. Couldn't you just find out some things he likes, so I know what to talk to him about? Pretty please? Just for me?'

'Oh, jeez.' Callum rolled his eyes. 'All right then. But only if you do the same for me one day!'

'Aha!' Sophie jumped on the comment. 'So who have *you* fallen for?'

Callum shrugged. 'No one. I don't do all that romance mush.' But Sophie noticed the muscle twitching in her friend's jaw. Was he fibbing to her? Before she could ask, he'd started to walk away.

Boys are such a mystery, she thought, shaking her head. Not the only mystery – Katy was an odd one, too. But she was determined to find out Katy's secret, whatever it was.

The elf warrior slashed at the approaching horde of skeletons, its gleaming sword sending blue light arcing through the forest.

'Back off, fiends!' Callum pounded the keyboard wildly. The computer speakers crackled with the sound of bones falling lifelessly to the floor.

'Can we play bowling again?' Sophie was near the bedroom window looking through his collection of games. She and Callum had tiptoed away, back down the corridor to the safety of his room. As she glanced up, she saw something running along the top of the fence outside. For a moment she thought it was a cat, then it sat up and looked at her with bright eyes, and she saw its large, black, bushy tail.

'Oh!' she exclaimed.

'What?'

'It's that squirrel again . . . the black one.'

'A black squirrel?' Callum didn't look up. 'You must be imagining it. Black squirrels don't live in England.'

'I'm not imagining it. This one is definitely black. Come and see for yourself.'

'Hang on, Sophie, I'm just about to level up.'

'Well, if you don't believe me . . . '

Callum sighed, pressed pause and came over. Together they knelt on the bed and looked down into the garden. The squirrel glared back at them.

'Hey, you're right,' said Callum. 'That's a black squirrel.'

'See, I told you. Look at the way it's staring at us.'

'How weird. We should write to *National Geographic*.'

Callum pressed his face close to the window. 'Have you seen it before?'

Sophie nodded. The squirrel was gazing directly at her. It was spooky . . . but fascinating at the same time. Did she dare tell Callum what she really thought?

'Actually, I think it's following me,' she admitted.

Callum laughed. 'Why don't you ask it what it wants, then?'

Sophie laughed, too. 'I know it's not really, don't worry. You'd have to be crazy to think a squirrel was following you around . . . ' She tailed off as she remembered her grandmother. 'Still, we could try!' She tapped on the glass. 'Come here, little squirrel! Come on.'

The squirrel cocked its head on one side.

'It's fearless, isn't it?' Callum unlatched the window and pushed it open. The smell of the sea mixed with the scent of jasmine floated in, and Sophie shivered suddenly. She stretched out her hand. In the moonlight the ring seemed to glow. She beckoned to the squirrel. For a moment she felt as if there was some kind of connection between them – but then the squirrel jumped down from the fence and vanished in the darkness.

'We scared him off,' said Callum, shrugging. 'Oh well ...' He leaned out to shut the window, then jumped back. 'Whoa!'

Sophie spotted a small, sleek black head pop up. The squirrel clambered up on to the windowsill, his big bright eyes watching Sophie closely. He sat there, twitching as if he was waiting for her to speak.

Slowly, Sophie held out her hand. The squirrel leaned forwards too. It stretched out its nose and gently touched her ring with it.

'That's amazing!' Callum whispered.

Sophie couldn't think of a word to say. She moved her hand to the left, and the squirrel followed. She lifted her fingers through the air, and the squirrel stood on its hind legs, its ears perked up and its tail quivering. Sophie slowly moved to stroke its head. She was sure the squirrel wouldn't let her touch it, but to her amazement it remained still, its eyes half closed as if in contentment, as she ran her hand over its silky fur.

'I hate to break the moment,' Callum said eventually. 'This is really cool, but you probably ought to let it go now. I mean, it might have fleas or something.'

'I suppose you're right.' Sophie drew her hand back, still gazing at the squirrel. Callum flapped at it gently. The animal gave him a look of disdain.

'You better be off, little fellow,' said Sophie.

Immediately, the squirrel turned and scampered across the windowsill. They leaned over and watched it leave, down the drainpipe till it disappeared in the shadows.

'It's almost as if it understands you,' Callum murmured. Sophie bit her lip. That's just what she'd been thinking.

'Oh my god, that test was so hard!' Sophie could hear Erin's voice ahead of her, echoing down the corridor as they made their way to the lunch hall. 'Don't you think, Katy?'

Sophie sped up. Her friends didn't seem to have noticed she wasn't with them; their backs formed a wall of red and grey uniforms, with Erin's blonde hair and Katy's black hair in the middle. Another time, she would have been worried about being left out. But now she was more interested in uncovering what was really going on with Katy Gibson.

'Don't worry, Erin!' Katy said with a laugh. 'I'm sure you'll have aced it.' She added, 'Oh, by the way, you know that strawberry lip-gloss of mine that you love? I found a spare tube when I finished unpacking – so now you can have your own!'

Erin gasped. 'Katy, that's so nice of you!'

Katy paused and pulled her school bag round to look into it. 'It's in here somewhere … Oh!' she exclaimed, her expression changing suddenly. She hesitated, then said, 'I think I've left my pencil case in the dorm. I'd better go up and get it.'

Sophie opened her mouth in surprise, then closed it again. She'd seen Katy using her pencil case in the last lesson and knew she hadn't been up to the dorm since. She was lying! But why?

'I'll see you in the dining hall, Erin,' Katy said, turning back towards Sophie.

'I'll save you a seat!' Erin waved.

Sophie backed against the wall. Katy didn't see her as she pushed through the crowd of boys and girls. Her heart beating fast, Sophie followed the other girl, craning around people to keep her in view. When Katy glanced back, she quickly stepped to the side, pretending to be interested in the lists of music exams on the notice-board. Out of the corner of her eye, she watched as Katy stopped and balanced her bag on her knee, rummaging inside. She pulled out her phone, and, as she did so, something small and silver fell out of her bag on to the floor.

Sophie turned round to see what it was, but, before she could, Callum, who had been hovering nearby, swooped and picked it up.

'Uh – I think you dropped this,' he said, holding it out to Katy.

'Oh!' Sophie saw Katy go pink as she took it. 'Oh, my money . . . Oh, thank you. Thank you.'

'No problem,' Callum said with a shy grin, backing away. 'It was only 5p.'

'Thanks anyway,' Katy shouted after him. Then she hurried off down the corridor and Sophie headed after her, determined not to let her out of her sight for a second. Katy went into a side corridor and Sophie followed, careful to stay at a distance in case Katy saw her. But Katy went on and turned the corner at the end. Sophie tiptoed up and peered round it.

Katy was leaning against the wall with her back to her. She had her phone out and was speaking into it.

'Yeah ... sorry ... I was with some people ...' She hesitated and dropped her voice very low. Sophie caught a few words. '... don't want to ... do I have to? ... Mum ...'

So she was talking to her mother. Sophie felt more and more puzzled.

'I hate this. I hate being here,' Katy said louder. She listened for a moment. 'It's so hard because these girls are ... Yeah. I know. OK. I'll do it.' Sophie couldn't make out all of the next sentence, but then she caught some words that sent a shiver over her. 'They're OK, quite nice ... but Erin ... witch.'

Sophie pulled back, breathless with shock. So Katy was smarming up to Erin and then being nasty about her behind her back! A hot wave of anger surged through her. How *dare* Katy act like that? Erin was the nicest, sweetest person.

Quick footsteps broke in on her thoughts, and, before she had a chance to move, Katy rounded the corner, almost bumping into her.

'Oh!' Katy gasped.

Sophie jolted away from her.

Katy's look of surprise turned to anger. 'Were you listening to my conversation?' she demanded.

'N – no. I – I just wondered if you were OK. Because,' Sophie added, gaining confidence, 'this isn't the way to the dining hall.'

Katy blinked. 'Oh. Well. I … I'm still finding my way round.' She moved past Sophie. 'Thanks for the help.'

'No problem,' Sophie called after her, watching Katy stride away. There had definitely been a flicker of guilt passing over her face. Not surprising, after calling Erin a witch.

Reluctantly, Sophie began to walk back down the corridor behind Katy, biting her tongue so as not to make a big scene by standing up for Erin.

As soon as they walked into the lunch hall Erin saw them, jumped up and waved. 'Hey, Katy! I saved you a seat next to me.'

'Oh, thanks!' Katy grinned as she threaded her way through the tables. She gave Erin a big hug as she got there. 'You're a star!'

How two-faced! Sophie thought. *One minute she's a witch, now she's a star.*

Sophie was glad Erin didn't speak to her; she thought she would've blurted out everything she'd just heard. Instead, she pulled out a seat at the far end of the table and pretended to be very interested in her fruit yoghurt while Katy produced the lip-gloss and Erin squealed in delight.

'Thanks, Katy! You're the best,' said Erin, and Sophie cringed.

'So, girls,' Katy demanded, beckoning the others in with a cheeky grin, 'how are your love lives?'

Sophie raised her eyebrows. The moody, nasty Katy who'd been on the phone to her parents seemed to have magically vanished.

Erin made a face. 'I've not heard from Mark in ages!

Three whole days. I was worrying about it all through the test.'

'Oh no! But Mark's really into you!' Lauren exclaimed. 'Don't you think, Katy?'

'Yeah, he's just being a boy,' said Katy, rolling her eyes. Everyone except Erin and Sophie giggled.

'I hope so, Katy ... ' Erin sighed, hunching over. 'Because it's, like, seriously affecting my work. I haven't even started the Science project. I mean, how can I observe tomato plants when I've got Mark on my mind?'

Katy nodded. 'They should set us Science projects on observing boys – we'd definitely hand that in on time!'

Erin laughed.

'What about you, Katy?' said Kaz teasingly. 'Who do you fancy?'

Katy wriggled and blushed. Sophie glanced up at her curiously.

'Oh, well ... there's one boy. I thought he was kind of a geek at first, but now I like him.' Katy looked directly at Sophie. 'Callum Pearce.'

117

The others swapped glances, and Lauren and Joanna giggled. Sophie's heart sank. Callum was the only one of her friends who hadn't fallen under Katy's spell. Besides, Katy was so two-faced . . . she hated the thought of Callum getting hurt.

'Take a ticket and get in line,' said Kaz, with an awkward smile.

'Oh, you like him?' Katy raised her eyebrows. 'Sorry. I didn't know.'

Kaz shrugged. 'That's OK. Everyone's got the Callum bug . . . well, nearly everyone.'

Katy licked her lips and leaned in, her eyes shining. 'I've got a cool idea,' she said in a low voice. 'Erin, you know the spell you did on Mark? How about we all get together tonight and cast a love spell on Callum? Let's try and get him to notice us. After all,' she added, her eyes fixed on Erin's face, 'your spell seemed to work.'

Sophie felt the corners of her mouth turn down. Not *another* midnight party! Her friends were all planning things without her, and now they were going to take Callum away from her too? It wasn't fair. They were all acting as if she didn't exist.

She realised everyone was looking at her.

'You could get it, couldn't you, Sophie?' said Jo. 'You see him all the time.'

'Huh?'

'A hair from Callum's head, so we can do the spell,' Lauren said. 'Please, Soph?'

'Um … I'll try,' said Sophie. *But not very hard*, she added to herself.

'Sophie doesn't get the Callum thing,' said Lauren with a giggle.

'But I know who you *do* fancy, Soph,' Kaz added in her usual loud voice. 'Ashton!'

All the girls' heads swivelled towards Katy. Sophie looked at Katy nervously, hoping she wouldn't tell him.

Katy shrugged. 'Got to be honest, Sophie, you're wasting your time.'

'Oh, really?' said Sophie. 'What do you mean by that?'

'I just don't really think you're his type.' The corner of Katy's mouth twitched in what looked like a superior smile.

119

Sophie's eyes widened in hurt shock. Two-faced Katy didn't think Sophie was good enough for her brother!

I could splurge your secrets right now! Sophie thought. *Then you'd stop smiling.* Her hands balled into fists beneath the dining hall table. She was bigger than that, she reminded herself. She wouldn't stoop to Katy's level.

Besides, Sophie wanted to get to the bottom of things before saying anything to anyone else. She gave Katy her best forced smile.

'I understand,' she said sweetly. 'Thanks for the tip.'

It was the best acting Sophie had ever done in her life.

That evening, after dinner, Sophie was sitting in the school library, looking out of the ground floor window over the courtyard. She was meant to be writing up her tomato plant project – but she was really thinking about the Gibsons. How could gorgeous Ashton have such a horrible sister? Katy had seemed so sweet when she'd first arrived; how could Sophie have been this wrong about her?

She shivered as an unexpected draught caught the back of her neck. The library was huge and shadowy, with tall wooden shelves reaching to the ceiling, where the dustiest old books were kept. The ornate iron vents looked impressive, but they made the library very cold. Sophie got up, meaning to go over and warm herself by one of the old Victorian radiators.

As she passed the window, a movement outside caught her eye. A figure had come out of the back doors of the school and, with a quick glance to each side, was hurrying across the courtyard. It was Katy. As Sophie watched, she disappeared through the doors of the Science block.

Sophie stared. The Science block was out of bounds at this time of night, and she doubted Katy was just keen to finish off her coursework – from what Sophie's mother had said, she couldn't care less. This had to be investigated!

Sophie rushed out of the library and headed across the yard. She remembered that the labs were always locked at night; Katy might be able to get into the block but what would she do once she was in there?

'Weirder and weirder,' she murmured to herself, as she followed Katy through the big glass doors.

Sophie tiptoed along the corridor, past Year 7's displays of pressed flowers – and stopped as she spotted Katy at the door of the Chemistry lab. She was trying the handle. The door rattled: locked. Sophie got ready to hide – she didn't want Katy turning round and bumping into her again.

But instead, Katy reached into her blazer pocket and pulled out a large key. It was made of dull metal and had irregular teeth. It wasn't like any key that Sophie had ever seen before. Katy slid the key into the lock and turned it. The door opened with a click, and she slipped through the gap.

For a moment, Sophie was frozen with astonishment. How had Katy managed to get the key to the lab? Then curiosity overtook her. She hurried to the door, catching it just before it swung shut, and cautiously peered around it.

Katy was on the far side of the room, at the store cupboard where all the dangerous chemicals were kept. As Sophie watched, she slid the same key into the store cupboard lock and turned it. The door opened, revealing rows of jars and bottles.

Where did she get that key? Sophie thought. It looked as if it could open any door in the world. She crept softly into the room, ducked down behind the work bench, and peered over the top.

Katy reached into the cupboard and brought out a cardboard box, which she placed on the teacher's desk. She opened her bag and retrieved something that looked like a water bottle, but the liquid inside was murky and bubbling. She unscrewed it and poured out a drop into the box, and Sophie heard a fizzing, popping sound. Then – to Sophie's amazement – Katy bent over the box and began to chant strange words, while making passes with her hands. Her voice was low, but Sophie could just hear her.

'*Umbra aut luce, die aut nocte, veritas pateat,*' Katy whispered. And then the word 'witch'.

As soon as she said 'witch' there was a gentle

sighing noise, and a cloud of purple vapour puffed out of the box and swirled in the air. Strange shapes and colours danced in it.

My grandmother was right! Witches do exist! Sophie gasped as the realisation hit her: *Witches exist, and Katy's one of them!*

Katy jumped at the sound of Sophie's inhalation and turned round. 'Who's there?' she exclaimed.

There was no point hiding now. Sophie straightened up and pointed at the box with a trembling hand.

'I knew there was something wrong about you!' she cried. 'You're a witch!'

'What?' Katy laughed nervously. 'I don't know what you're talking about.' She tried to shield the box with her body, but the purple smoke still hung in the air.

'So what was that chanting? And the smoke?' Sophie backed away, her heart thumping. 'You were casting a spell! And not some silly romantic spell to make boys fall in love. You're a real witch!'

'No, of course I wasn't, I'm not. I was just – er – er . . .' Katy glanced anxiously at the box.

'Just what?! You're a witch, don't try to deny it!'

'You're being silly. Witches don't exist!' Katy said with a confident toss of her hair.

'That's it. You're lying.' Sophie backed towards the door. 'I'm going to tell my mum! No – the police! This has got to be a crime!'

'Whatever!' Katy raised her voice. 'You must be crazy. Witches don't exist, so how can I be one?'

'I don't care what you say! I had a bad feeling about you from the start,' Sophie said. 'All of a sudden you were magically Miss Popular – well, now I know how you did it! You're a mean witch and you're casting spells on my friends.' She turned to the door. 'I'm going to stop you.'

'No! Wait!' The terror in Katy's voice was so strong that Sophie turned back towards her. 'You mustn't tell anyone. I'm not a witch, I promise. I'm good!'

Sophie pulled the door open.

'Let me explain! Sophie, *please.*' Katy moved towards her, suddenly sounding desperate. All the cool confidence had evaporated. Sophie wavered, her hand resting on the handle. Katy's eyes pleaded with her.

But I've seen the proof with my own eyes, screeched a voice in Sophie's head. *She's not to be trusted!*

That was it. She headed out and down the corridor. She had almost reached the outside door when she heard Katy running after her. She spun round. The two girls stood face to face.

'OK, OK. You're right,' gasped Katy. Her face was white and she was trembling. 'Witches do exist!'

TEN

'Five minutes,' Sophie said. She gripped the door handle tightly so she could make a quick getaway. 'You've got five minutes to explain exactly what all this is about – before I tell the whole world what I know.'

Katy took a deep breath.

'Witches do exist,' said Katy flatly. 'Witches *do* exist – but I'm not one of them.'

Sophie stared at Katy, a flicker of unease passing over her. For some reason, she believed what Katy was saying.

'I'm the opposite. I'm a witch hunter.'

Sophie felt the blood drain from her face. 'A what?'

'A witch hunter. It's our duty to rid the world of witches.'

Sophie's mind was swirling. Duty? Rid the world? Witches? These didn't sound like the words a real person would use.

'I know it sounds strange to you, but it's the truth. I was destined to be a witch hunter from the moment I was born.' She stared at the ground, sounding tired and sad. 'That's why I'm here, at Turlingham.'

'I don't get it.' Sophie frowned. 'Why would you find an old witch in a school like this? Unless you mean one of the teachers—'

'You don't understand. Witches aren't all old women. A witch gets her power on her thirteenth birthday, and keeps on growing stronger with every year.' She shuddered. 'They become very, very dangerous.'

Sophie nodded uncertainly. Witches were bad, she knew that. All the stories she'd ever read said so anyway.

Katy continued, 'So my job is to go from school to school, hunting down new witches, before they become a threat.'

Seven schools in two years. It flashed through Sophie's mind.

'And there's a witch in Turlingham,' Katy continued, as matter-of-factly as if she were saying there was a bird in a tree. 'All I have to do now is find who it is. That's why I was doing that experiment.'

Sophie slowly let go of the door handle. *Is she crazy?* she wondered. But then what about her grandmother's letters? It couldn't just be a coincidence. Besides, she'd seen the magic with her own eyes.

'As soon as I find the witch, I'll be out of here. On to the next school,' Katy said quietly. 'I know I've made life uncomfortable for you. I didn't mean to. I just really needed all the girls to like me – it makes my job so much easier.'

Sophie took a deep breath, her mind working fast. The best thing she could do would be to help Katy, get her out of this school, and get everything back to normal.

'I'll help you,' she said.

Katy looked up, wide-eyed. 'You will?'

Sophie nodded slowly. 'Maybe you're crazy. But as soon as you find your witch, you'll leave, right?'

Katy nodded too, her eyes brimming with tears. Sophie felt a stab of guilt. *It must be awful to feel so unwelcome.* But Sophie had to stay strong!

'Good! As soon as you're out of here, my life will go back to normal. So, let's do it!'

Katy stared at her. 'You're sure? It can be dangerous, you know.'

'We find the witch and you leave.' Sophie stuck out her hand. 'That's all I'm interested in. Deal?'

After a long moment, Katy said, 'Deal,' and reached out to shake her hand.

Five hours later, Sophie was slinking down the moon-lit Year 9 corridor. She winced as the old floorboards squeaked under her feet, fighting the urge to turn round and run. She stared at the door of the Year 9 bathroom. There would be no going back once she'd opened it.

She braced herself and pushed it open.

A torch beam flashed into her eyes, blinding her. When her eyes had adjusted, she saw Katy in front of her. Katy gave her a cool nod before glancing out into the corridor.

'Follow me. Watch what I do.' She switched the torch off and led the way out.

'And hello to you too,' Sophie muttered under her breath. She followed, impressed despite herself. Katy seemed experienced at this. How many witches had she already caught?

As they crept along the corridor towards the dorms, Sophie found herself jumping at the slightest noise. Suddenly the school she was so familiar with was terrifying, like there was a witch lurking around every corner. Not to mention all the times she'd been in trouble already this year – and they weren't even at half term. *If Mrs Freeman catches me . . .* she thought. *Or Maggie . . . I could be suspended!*

Katy turned to her and said in a whisper, 'You need to know how to tell that someone's a witch. There are things to look out for.'

'Like a black cat and a pointy hat?' Sophie's nervous giggle died away as she saw Katy's deadly-serious expression in the torchlight.

'Not so obvious. First, witches always have an object they take with them everywhere. Can't bear to be parted from it.' She ticked the points off on her fingers. 'Second, they're good at reading people. Often one of the most popular people in the school. Third, they'll have a familiar – a pet. Or they'll be good with animals.' She glanced at Sophie. 'I have a few suspects in mind already.'

'Oh . . . good,' said Sophie faintly. Her mind was racing as she tried to think who fitted the description. Then she remembered Katy's phone call to her parents. *She can't think Erin is the witch, surely!* Sophie thought, not daring to say the words out loud.

'The next step is to test them.' Katy held up a box and shook it. It looked like the one she was looking at in the Science lab and it sounded as if it had sand inside. 'These are iron filings – specially treated ones, of course. If the person we're tracking really is a witch, the filings will move into the shape of a crescent moon when they come near her.'

They were at the door of the Year 10 dorm. Katy rested her hand on it. She glanced at Sophie and put her finger to her lips. Then she pushed the door open.

Sophie followed her inside. Six beds were filled with the shapes of sleeping girls.

'Watch me,' Katy mouthed. She edged her way between the beds and stopped beside a humped, pink duvet. Sophie recognised the girl asleep under it as Susie Maitland, a keen rider who kept her pony in Turlingham's stables. *Could she really be a witch?* Sophie wondered.

Katy opened the box and tipped a pinch of iron filings into the palm of her hand. She tossed the filings on to the floor. Sophie peered over her shoulder. In the moonlight, the iron filings lay still.

'Nothing,' Katy whispered.

'You're surprised?' Sophie whispered back.

Katy beckoned her to the door. They tiptoed out into the corridor. Katy faced her and said in a low voice, 'No, I'm not surprised. I had to rule Susie out ... but I'm almost positive the witch is Erin Best.'

Sophie felt her face grow red with anger. 'Erin's my friend.'

Katy raised her hands defensively. 'Remember what I said about witches being really popular, friendly people? It's because they can read other people's emotions well. And wasn't it Erin who suggested putting a spell on Mark Little? A spell that actually worked?'

Sophie frowned, not liking to admit that Katy had a point.

'Do you know if she has a pet at home?' Katy went on.

Sophie shivered suddenly, remembering Bugsy the Labrador puppy.

'Well?' Katy stared at her.

'N – no. I don't think she does,' Sophie managed. *Come on, Sophie,* she told herself, *don't be silly. Erin isn't a witch!*

'Go ahead and test her if you want,' she whispered, trying to sound casual. 'It'll just rule her out, you'll see.'

'We'll soon find out,' replied Katy, shaking the box.

Silently, she pushed open the door to the Year 9 dorm. Sophie watched, hugging herself, from the doorway as Katy walked over to Erin's bed. Katy took a pinch of iron filings and scattered them on the floor. Sophie closed her eyes. She couldn't bear to watch. *Please, don't let my friend be a witch!* she thought.

Katy sighed. Sophie opened her eyes, quickly. The iron filings lay still and unmoving on the ground. She couldn't help smiling.

'Told you,' she whispered to Katy. 'Why are you looking so disappointed, anyway?'

Katy shook her head as she rejoined her. 'I'm not convinced. It could still be Erin.'

Sophie scowled. Katy added hurriedly, 'I hope I'm wrong! I like Erin too. But if she's a witch ... well, it doesn't matter if I like her or not.'

'Your own iron filings showed she's not a witch!'

'Sometimes witches carry magnets to hide their powers, and that stops the iron filings working. If Erin guessed we were on to her, she could have hidden a magnet somewhere.' She hesitated and

135

glanced back towards Erin. 'Maybe we should search her.'

'No! She'll wake up.'

'You're right.' Katy nodded. 'We'll leave it – for now.'

Sophie covered her mouth as she yawned. She glanced at her watch.

'It's nearly two,' she whispered to Katy.

'We've got to work faster.' Katy bit her nail. 'Let's split up – here, take some iron filings.' She tipped some into Sophie's cupped hand. 'I'm going to try the other Year 9 dorms. Meet you back here in an hour.'

Sophie stood for a moment, wondering what to do. She didn't like the idea of going around testing people while they slept – it felt sneaky. But if they were going to catch the witch, there wasn't any choice. She headed towards the Year 11 dorm and pushed open the door, glad it didn't creak.

Her attention was drawn by a faint snore in one of the beds. She noticed a printed list pinned above it: the heading TURLINGHAM ACADEMY RULES was visible in the moonlight. It could only be Maggie Millar.

Sophie stared at Maggie, trying to imagine her on a

broomstick, cackling as she flew across the night sky. She was certainly horrible enough to be a witch. And if she *was* a witch and Katy could get rid of her ... that would kill two birds with one stone!

Sophie crept towards Maggie's bed. The floorboards squeaked under her feet and one of the girls rolled over with a sigh. Sophie froze. She caught a glimpse of herself in the mirror on the wall. Suddenly she thought: *This is crazy!* What was she doing in the middle of the night, sneaking up to her fellow students' beds? There couldn't be any such thing as witches. Surely there couldn't.

Behind her, one of the girls coughed loudly in her sleep. Sophie jumped. She watched in horror as the filings flew up and scattered all over the room.

'Huh – who's that?' The girl who had coughed sat up with a yawn. Sophie dropped flat on the floor and lay there, her heart beating wildly, hoping the girl wouldn't look down and see her.

She tensed herself, ready to bolt for the exit. Then, out of the corner of her eye, she saw something move on the floor. She froze.

At first she thought it was an army of ants, but then she realised it was the iron filings. They were moving across the floor towards her, as if blown by a breeze. The powdery filings clustered into the shape of a crescent moon, with the horns of the moon pointing directly at Sophie.

Sophie's mouth fell open as she stared at the accusing horns. She realised what this meant.

'Oh no,' she whispered. Suddenly it all seemed so obvious. Her 'lucky motto' that made things happen, her grandmother's letters, the ring she'd got for her thirteenth birthday, with its stone shaped like a crescent moon ... How could she not have seen it?

Her head spun as she remembered all the things that hadn't made sense at the time. The lighthouse beacon coming on, Maggie looking right through her, the lucky branch that had broken the window and distracted her ... all those things had happened right after she'd asked the Forces of the Earth to help her.

Witches *did* exist – and *she* was one of them.

She, Sophie Morrow, was the witch at Turlingham!

'YOU!' exclaimed a furious, familiar voice. Maggie

was sitting up, fumbling for the light switch. 'You are in so much trouble!'

For once, Sophie completely agreed with her – but she didn't stop to say so. She just ran.

ELEVEN

Sophie pelted down the back stairs, her sides aching as she tried to keep ahead of Maggie. *I'm a witch, I'm a witch, I'm a witch!* whirled through her mind as she ran. *What am I going to do?* Behind her, she could hear Maggie panting for breath, her feet thumping down the steps.

At the bottom of the stairs Sophie shot the bolts of the door, wrenched it open and ran out into the night air. In front of her were the woods that backed on to the school grounds. She glanced over her shoulder.

Maggie was nowhere to be seen. Right on the edge of the woods was a tall pine tree. Sophie ran towards it and tried to climb up. The rough bark hurt her fingers as she slid back down. She was about to try again when a small dark figure bounded down the trunk to her. It was the black squirrel.

The squirrel leapt on to her shoulder, brushing its tail comfortingly against her skin. Then it darted to the ground and ran into the trees, pausing on the edge of the woods to look back at her.

Does it want me to follow it? Sophie wondered. She risked a glimpse behind her. To her horror, Maggie was coming out of the door.

'I can see you!' she heard her yell.

Sophie made a snap decision. She raced after the squirrel, into the woods.

As she went into the trees, the moonlight was blotted out by the branches. She stumbled in the dark across the uneven ground. Looking back once more, she saw Maggie silhouetted on the edge of the woods, before she plunged in after her.

The squirrel flung itself from branch to branch,

finally stopping on one which hung invitingly low. Sophie scrambled on to it. To her surprise, she found another handhold immediately and was able to pull herself up. The squirrel led her up the tree, from hand-hold to handhold, until she was perched high above the ground, on a flattened branch. She pulled her legs up and sat, listening out for Maggie and panting for breath.

'Thanks, little guy!' she whispered to the squirrel.

Below, she heard Maggie crashing through the undergrowth. 'Come back! You can't escape!' Maggie's voice died away in the distance. Sophie clutched her knees and sat, shivering.

After a while she heard Maggie thumping back through the trees below her. 'You'll regret this, Sophie Morrow!' she shouted. Maggie had clearly given up for the night, and, after a long moment, the door to the school slammed.

Silence returned to the woods, but Sophie's head was still whirling. As she sat on the branch, she tried to make sense of what had happened. As she thought back over the days since her thirteenth birthday, it all seemed so obvious. She bit her nails, thinking hard. But wicked witches were out of storybooks, they couldn't be real! Maybe she was just panicking, maybe she'd let Katy's wild stories get to her . . .

A leaf floated past, spinning slowly as it fell. Sophie stared at it. *If I really am a witch, I should be able to prove it.*

'Forces of the Earth,' she whispered, 'make that leaf stop falling.' She pointed her ring finger at the leaf, willing it to stay still. The leaf slowed, then stopped, hanging in mid-air, twirling on the spot in the gentle breeze. Sophie gasped out loud.

With her other hand, she plucked it out of the air. She turned it this way and that, marvelling at her own power. But what would she do with that power? Did she have to use it for evil, just because she was a witch?

There was a scuffle above her, and more leaves fell. The squirrel came scampering down the trunk. Sophie smiled despite her worry.

'Hey,' she whispered. 'Thanks for saving me from Maggie the Monster. You must be my pet. I mean, my familiar.'

The squirrel dipped its head as if it was nodding. She held out her arm and the little creature leapt on to it, pausing only to touch her ring with its nose.

'I suppose you knew I was a witch all along, didn't you? I'm sorry I didn't get it till now.' She gently stroked its head. 'You need a proper name ... How about Gally?' She smiled. 'I'm glad you're here, Gally. At least there's one person I can talk to about all this craziness! Even if you're not exactly a person.'

She fell silent as a thought struck her. It wasn't just Gally she could talk to, she remembered. *I have to warn you of something: witches are real.* Her grandmother knew about witches. She'd tried to warn her – but of what? Was the warning that she was turning into a witch? Or was there some other danger out there? After all, back in the school, Katy was busy trying to track down the hidden witch. Sophie gulped.

She was the witch Katy was hunting.

Sophie stifled a yawn as she hurried along the corridor towards the dining hall. She turned the corner, and bumped right into Maggie.

145

'Aha!' Maggie exclaimed, pinning her against the wall. 'I was looking for you!'

'M-me? Why?' Sophie looked up at her, hoping she didn't appear as nervous as she felt.

'Because I want to know what you were doing sneaking round my dorm last night!'

'What do you mean, Maggie?' Sophie opened her eyes wide and smiled as innocently as she could. 'What would I have been doing in your dorm?'

'I'm glad you asked,' Maggie retorted. She opened her fist to show a handful of iron filings. 'Do *these* refresh your memory?'

Sophie swallowed hard. Had Maggie seen the iron filings move?

Maggie leaned in and dropped her voice to a threatening hiss.

'I've been weighing the iron filings in the Science lab and I'm sure some are missing. It all makes sense: you're stealing school supplies and selling them at a profit!' Sophie's jaw dropped and Maggie grinned triumphantly. 'Yeah, that's right – I've guessed it all.

THE WITCH OF TURLINGHAM ACADEMY

You picked the wrong prefect to mess with, Sophie Morrow.'

Sophie choked on an incredulous giggle.

'Um, Maggie, I don't know what you're talking about. I've been in bed all night, sound asleep. Why would I want to sell *iron filings*?'

'You're lying!' Maggie shook her fist. 'I may not have proof right now, but I'm going to get it and then I'm going to make sure they expel you. This school has a zero-tolerance policy towards theft.'

'Whatever,' Sophie interrupted. She felt lightheaded with lack of sleep and delayed shock, and she could hardly believe she was talking so confidently. 'It doesn't really matter what you think, because, like you said, you can't prove a thing. Not that there's anything to prove.'

She pushed past Maggie and hurried off. Behind her, she heard Maggie shout, 'You can't get away with everything!'

Sophie almost danced down the corridor. Witch or not, it felt really good to get one over Maggie! She swung round the corner and found herself facing a big, bright poster on the wall, advertising the Welcome Back Dance.

'Oh, brilliant!' she exclaimed aloud. So her mother and Mr Pearce had definitely decided on it. She glanced down the corridor and spotted Ashton Gibson, looking as handsome as ever. Without thinking, she raised her hand in a wave and called out, 'Hi, Ashton!' The next second she couldn't believe what she'd done – what if he blanked her? What if Katy had told him that she liked him? What if he laughed at her?

But Ashton grinned and sped up, weaving his way through the crowd until he reached her.

'Hi yourself. What's up?'

Sophie felt a huge smile spread over her face. *Go with it*, she thought. She gestured at the poster on the wall.

'Just looking at this. Are you going?'

'Hmm, it depends.'

'On what?'

'On who else might be going.' He gave her a flash of his green eyes.

Sophie squeezed her lips together to stop herself grinning like an idiot. 'You mean you haven't got a date?' she asked.

'Not yet.'

'Me neither.' Sophie crossed her fingers behind her back.

Ashton glanced at the poster again.

'Well, well, two people without dates. What if we went together?'

'That would be ... great!' Sophie managed to say.

'Cool.' Ashton shifted his bag strap and grinned at her. 'So, I'll see you later?'

'Definitely. Definitely!'

Ashton gave her a dazzling smile and strolled off. Sophie leaned back against the wall. She waited until he was well out of earshot to let out a squeal of delight.

'I can't believe it! Ashton Gibson asked me out!'

It was almost enough to make her forget she was a witch.

TWELVE

'Now, remember, Sophie, if you start feeling uncomfortable we can leave at once,' said Mrs Morrow as she led the way across the car park towards the Bowden Psychiatric Hospital. It was Friday lunch hour and Sophie's mum had finally given in to her pleading and agreed to take her to visit her grandmother.

'Mum, there's no need to worry,' Sophie said. 'She's my grandmother, after all. It's going to be fine.'

All the same, she was glad she had a big bunch of flowers to hold on to. As they went up the gravel path, between the pretty flower beds, she peeped from behind her bouquet at the people strolling in the garden. They seemed happy, she thought, and her spirits rose a little.

'Hello, Mrs Morrow!' The receptionist greeted them with a sunny smile as they came through the sliding glass doors. 'You're later than usual.'

'Hello, Sumira. Yes, I decided to bring my daughter along. It's her lunch hour.'

The receptionist smiled at Sophie.

'Mrs Poulter will love those flowers. Go right on through.'

Sophie smiled back. As they walked away she whispered to her mother, 'I didn't know you came here every week!'

Sophie's mum looked a little embarrassed.

'Well, I couldn't abandon the poor woman. I made sure she was admitted to a hospital close by, so I could visit regularly. I'm sorry I didn't tell you, but . . . '

'It's OK. I understand. I'm really glad you visit her,' said Sophie, squeezing her mum's hand. Another thought came to her: so her father wasn't visiting – he'd abandoned his mother just as he had his wife and daughter.

'I'd like to come every week, too,' she said.

Her mother smiled at her. 'Let's see how this visit goes first, eh?'

As they walked on, Sophie remembered her grandmother's letter again – *I have to warn you of something: witches are real.* For the first time, she realised that sentence could mean anything. Her grandmother might know Sophie was a witch, or she might not. She might be a witch herself . . . or, worse, what if she was a witch hunter? Would she kiss Sophie on the cheek or throw iron filings in her face?

Her mother stopped outside a door marked MRS LOVEDAY POULTER. Glancing down, she put a hand on Sophie's shoulder.

'I know how important this is to you, but remember, she is very ill,' she said gently. 'Don't be too disappointed if the meeting isn't . . . all that you hoped it would be.'

Sophie swallowed and nodded.

'Ready?'

'Yes.'

'Sure?'

'Sure.'

Sophie's mum knocked. After a few moments, a quavering voice called, 'Come in.'

Sophie followed her mother inside, clutching the flowers tightly. On the other side of the room, a television was on and a chair was facing it. Sophie could see a person with white hair sitting in it, their back to the door. A walking stick leaned against the arm rest.

Her mum went over to the woman and smiled down at her. 'It's me again, Loveday. I've brought a visitor this time.'

Sophie watched nervously as a wrinkled hand reached out from the chair and picked up the remote control. The television winked off. Then the figure turned and stared at her. The woman had a rosy, wrinkled face, and Sophie's stomach jumped as she realised she had the same warm brown eyes as her father.

The woman's face broke into a broad smile and she felt for her stick. Sophie's mother handed it to her. The woman heaved herself up from her chair, leaning on the stick with one gnarled hand, and held out the other to Sophie.

'Sophie! My granddaughter. At last,' she said warmly. 'Come here and give me a hug.'

Sophie went awkwardly across the room and allowed her grandmother to hug her. Just as she'd begun to feel comfortable, her grandmother let go and held her at arm's length, studying her carefully. Sophie was reminded of the searching way that Katy's parents had looked at her. But her grandmother's gaze fell almost at once to her hand.

'Ah, the ring.' She lifted Sophie's hand and studied the jewellery, turning it this way and that so the crescent moon flashed in the light. 'Do you like it?'

Sophie nodded. 'It's perfect.'

'Good.' Her grandmother's eyes twinkled. 'What beautiful flowers you've brought me! Tamsin, do you think you could find a vase for them? Over there, in the cupboard above the sink.'

'Of course.' Sophie's mother took the flowers and went over to the corner where the cupboard was.

Sophie's grandmother sat carefully in the chair and drew Sophie down to perch on the arm next to her.

'So ... ' she said thoughtfully. 'Thirteen. It's a difficult age, I remember well. But an exciting one, too.' She gave a strange, knowing smile. 'How have you been feeling recently? Any ... changes? Have you noticed any differences? Some new friends, perhaps?'

Sophie nodded, thinking of Gally as well as Katy.

'Now take it easy on her,' Sophie's mother said with a nervous smile as she returned with the flowers in a vase. She placed it on the windowsill.

'It's OK, Mum,' said Sophie, looking into her grandmother's warm eyes. 'Could you ... leave us alone for a few moments, please?'

Her mother looked worried. 'I ... well, OK. Five minutes.' She moved towards the door and beckoned Sophie over. 'There's an alarm by the window,' she said under her breath. 'Press it if you feel the need, or if your grandmother starts to feel ill.'

Sophie nodded and returned to her grandmother. She sat down in the window seat, facing her. Her grandmother waited silently until the door had clicked shut. Then she sat up straight, her eyes flashed with intelligence and she smiled.

'That's better. Let me have a good look at you!' She reached over and took Sophie's chin, examining her carefully. 'You remind me of your father.'

Sophie pulled away, feeling slightly annoyed. But perhaps her grandmother didn't realise he had betrayed them as well as her, she thought.

'So, I expect you know you're a witch by now, don't you?'

Sophie gasped. She hadn't expected her to be so blunt. But then she nodded, feeling oddly comforted at the matter-of-fact way her grandmother had said it.

'Good. This,' she lifted Sophie's hand and turned the ring so it flashed in the light, 'is your Source.' She reached into the collar of her shirt and pulled out a necklace with a star-shaped pendant on the chain. 'This is mine . . . but I can't use it any more.'

'Use it?' asked Sophie.

'You need your Source to cast spells. Never be parted from it. Did you first put it on on your thirteenth birthday?'

Sophie shook her head. 'I only found it a few days ago.'

Her grandmother sighed. 'What a pity. That means you might take a while to develop your full gifts. They may even never fully develop.'

Sophie wasn't sure if she was pleased or disappointed. She turned the ring – her Source – on her finger, trying to take all this in.

'Of course, your mother knows nothing of this – and we need to keep it that way, for her own safety.' Her grandmother patted her hand. 'I have no doubt you're finding it a bit of a shock.'

Sophie half smiled. 'Just a bit.'

'Well, there certainly is a lot to explain. But don't worry, I am on your side. I am a witch too.' She hesitated. 'And so is your father.'

'My father?' Sophie looked at her in shock. 'Does Mum know about *that*?'

Her grandmother shook her head.

'Your mother is human. She doesn't know anything about witches. Your father decided that was for the best.'

Sophie raised an eyebrow. Her grandmother went on, her voice sad and thoughtful as she gazed at the flowers they'd brought. 'He was deeply in love with your mother, you see, and he just wanted a normal life for all three of you, without the ... risks that finally drove him away.'

Sophie was speechless. *Drove* him away – so he hadn't chosen to leave them. He had cared, after all. She felt a flood of happiness and realised she was in danger of crying. It had hurt so much to think he'd never cared – what a relief to discover he'd loved them after all.

'Do you know where he is? If he's – if he's alive?' she finally managed to say.

Her grandmother shook her head sadly. 'I don't know, my dear. I just don't know.'

Sophie's face fell. Her grandmother leaned towards her and placed a hand on hers. 'But I know this much: something has happened to keep him away. He would never, ever have left you and your mother if he hadn't been forced to. He loved you both so much.'

The tears finally pricked Sophie's eyes. Her grandmother hurried on.

'We haven't much time. Now, this is very, very important. You must stay away from witch hunters. They demagicked me so that I am no longer able to use my powers, or cast a spell.' She looked pained as she spoke. 'Your so-called friend Katy Gibson – keep away from her. Far away.'

'How do you know about Katy?'

Her grandmother smiled quickly. 'I sent Corvis to keep an eye on you.'

Sophie followed her gaze, turned and glimpsed a large black bird in the branches of the cherry tree outside the window.

'The raven!' she exclaimed.

'That's right. But, Sophie, listen to me. You must keep away from the Gibson family.'

Sophie turned back to her grandmother.

'I don't mind staying away from Katy,' she said. After all, the only reason she'd agreed to help Katy was to get her out of school. 'But ... I don't have to stay away from Ashton Gibson too, do I?'

'Yes, you must. All the Gibsons are very, very danger-ous!' Her grandmother pressed her hand hard, looking fiercely into her eyes.

'It's just ... we have sort of a date ...' Sophie fal-tered.

Her grandmother jerked back as if she had been struck, the tic in her face jumping faster.

'With a witch hunter? Sophie, n-no! You c-can't possibly.' Her fingers bit into Sophie's hand. 'He'll demagick you ... or worse! You must stay far, *far* away from them!'

'But I don't—'

'You have to listen to me!' her grandmother went on, her voice shaking with passion. 'The Gibsons are lethal. You are in d-dreadful danger!'

'Grandma, let go, you're hurting me!' Sophie felt panic rise in her chest. She really did look insane.

'Not until you listen!'

Her grandmother lunged towards her and grabbed her shoulders, holding her firmly. Sophie let out a frightened gasp as her grandmother's weight pushed her backwards into the vase, which fell and smashed on the floor. She reached behind her and managed to find the alarm button. She pressed it hard. Distantly, she heard a buzzing.

'You're not leaving this room until you've promised not to see any of the Gibsons ever again!' Sophie was too terrified to reply. 'Promise!' Her grandmother shook her, staring fiercely into her face. 'Promise me!'

'Grandma, I – I—'

The door burst open and two young men in white coats rushed in, followed by Sophie's mother. Sophie pulled away as they leaned over her grandmother, saying, 'Easy, Mrs Poulter, you're scaring your grand-daughter.'

'The witch hunters!' her grandmother screamed, pushing them aside. 'Sophie, stay away from them!' She gasped as one of the men grabbed her arms and the other whipped out a syringe.

'Now, just keep calm.' He quickly injected her. Sophie watched, wide-eyed and horrified, as her grand-mother struggled furiously with the men. 'There, there, Mrs Poulter. The medicine will start working in a moment, then it will be time for your nap.'

Her mother was pale and shaking. She put an arm round Sophie's shoulder and led her out of the room. 'Sophie, I'm so sorry. I should never have brought you here. Are you OK, darling?'

Sophie nodded, though she felt close to tears as she rubbed the red marks on her skin. As they hurried down the corridor, she could hear her grandmother still desperately shouting: 'Stay away from them, Sophie, please!'

THIRTEEN

'Saturday at last!' Lauren sighed in delight as Sophie led the way through the door of the Seagull Café. She turned back to Katy. 'I've been waiting all week for my chocolate fondant milkshake.'

'It all looks amazing!' Katy agreed as she gazed at the rows of cakes and the menu of milkshake flavours. Sophie and Katy hadn't been alone together since Sophie had disappeared from their night errand with the iron filings. Katy hadn't said a word to her about her secret role as a witch hunter, and

Sophie wanted to keep it that way. *I need time to think!*

Sophie chose a milkshake and a cake, and hurried over to the table by the window. She glanced down inside her shoulder bag as she sat down: two bright black eyes peeped back up at her.

'Are you OK in there, Gally?' she whispered. As Katy came over with her tray, she quickly crumbled off a bit of her cake and dropped it into her bag. Gally pounced on it eagerly. Sophie looked up, met Katy's eyes and forced a smile. Katy smiled back warmly. Sophie noticed that she looked straight into her eyes and she didn't play with her hair like she used to. Why was she acting so confident when she knew Sophie could blow her secret at any moment?

'It's a pity I didn't see you last night,' Katy said to Sophie in a low voice as she sat down. 'I was really hoping we could test Erin again. Do you know what she's up to today? I'm worried she's on to us and is keeping her distance.'

'N-no, I don't think so,' Sophie said truthfully. She hoped her face didn't show how nervous she felt. It was easy enough to avoid Katy at night-time, but she couldn't just blank her during the day – or *everyone* would get suspicious. 'She had to see my mum for something.'

'What are you two gossiping about?' Kaz sat down next to them with her tray. 'Share!'

Sophie panicked for a moment, but then the bell at the door jingled. Sophie looked up to see Erin burst in. There were tears running down her face.

'Erin! What happened?' she exclaimed.

Erin rushed over to their table and sat down, still sobbing. Lauren and Jo turned round as they heard her, and came hurrying over from the counter.

Erin wept. 'The school called my p-parents, because I didn't do the Biology coursework – and my parents were soooo mad . . . They say if I don't get an A for the tomato project, I'll have to leave T-Turlingham and go back to America for good!'

There was a shocked silence around the table. The six girls stared at each other in horror – at least, five of them did. Sophie wasn't sure if Katy's expression was horror or relief.

'Oh, Erin!' Lauren broke the silence. 'But then we'll – we'll never see you again!' She began to sob too, and flung her arms around Erin, who cried even harder.

Sophie swallowed the lump in her throat. It would be awful if Erin was taken away from the school and she couldn't help feeling guilty, guessing that her own mother had placed the call to Erin's parents. Sometimes it sucked, being the daughter of a head teacher. She took Erin's shaking hand.

'Isn't there any way you could get an A?' she said hopefully. 'It's just looking at tomato plants and writing it up, isn't it?'

'But it's d-due Monday morning and I think the tomato plants are dead – at least, I don't *think* they're meant to be grey and c-crumbly . . . ' Erin wailed.

Sophie hugged her tight. 'Don't worry, Erin. I'll help you. There's no way you're leaving Turlingham.'

'Thanks, Soph.' Erin lifted her head and gave her a weak smile. 'You're a great friend . . . but what can you *do*?'

'I don't know, but I've always been good with

plants. I'll think of something,' Sophie promised. *There's got to be some magic that can fix this*, she thought to herself. *I won't let Erin go without a fight.*

She didn't dare check the expression on Katy's face.

'They do look pretty dead,' Sophie admitted, as she examined the tomato plants an hour later. She poked a stalk and it crumbled. 'Did you forget to water them recently?'

'Water them?' Erin said blankly.

'You didn't water them at all?! Oh Erin, no wonder they look dead.'

Erin's mouth wobbled.

'Don't worry,' Sophie said hastily. 'My mum has this great gardening book – she's always on about how useful it is. I'll just go and look up what it says about tomatoes.'

'OK.' Erin sniffed. 'I'll get my homework stuff.'

Sophie raced out of the Biology lab and back to her own cottage. She went to the potting shed and pulled open the door.

'I don't think any book is going to help those tomatoes, Gally,' she said to the squirrel as it poked its nose out of her bag. 'I think we need some kind of magic . . . but how are we going to do it?'

Gally jumped out of her bag and started nosing around the shelves. He dived in between her mum's old gardening gloves and her new trowel. Sophie bent down to watch him and saw a bag of fertiliser.

'Great idea, Gally!' she exclaimed, scooping up a handful. 'Earth, water, wind and fire. Oh Forces of the Earth, hear me,' she whispered to the fertiliser. 'Make Erin's tomato plants the best in the class!'

Putting it in a small flowerpot, she hurried back to the lab.

Erin looked up from her books as Sophie came in. 'Did you find anything?'

'I'm going to try some of Mum's fertiliser,' Sophie answered. She carried the plant over to the sink and mixed the fertiliser with tap water.

She gazed anxiously at the mixture. A slight rainbow sheen glinted on the muddy water. She poured it on to the dead stalks, and . . . nothing. Part of her had been hoping they would magically burst into life, but they looked just as dead as before.

Erin looked expectantly at her as she put them back on the windowsill.

'Now what?'

'Um . . . I think you should water them every hour,' said Sophie. 'You never know. It might help.'

She crossed her fingers behind her back as they left the lab. 'Oh Forces of the Earth, please don't muck this up.'

As she followed the rest of the class into the Biology lab on Monday morning, Sophie sneaked a glance at the row of tomato plants on the windowsill. She grinned to herself as she saw that one was several inches higher than the others and covered in glossy red fruit.

'I finished, I finished!' Erin bounded in and joined Lauren and Sophie at the work bench. 'I worked soooo hard. I don't think I've ever worked that hard in my life. And I finished writing up and handed it in last night!'

'Erin, well done!' Lauren exclaimed, giving her a hug.

'I knew you could do it!' Sophie beamed. She felt really pleased – she'd fixed the plants, but Erin had done the homework all on her own. 'Are those huge tomato plants yours?'

'Yes! Isn't it incredible? I watered them every hour, like you suggested, and they just grew so fast. Come and look, girls.' Erin rushed over to admire the plants, followed by Kaz, Joanna and Lauren.

Katy tapped Sophie's shoulder and leaned towards her.

'I smell witchcraft,' she whispered. 'How could she have brought those plants back from the dead just by watering, in two days? It's not possible.'

Sophie swallowed. Perhaps her miracle cure hadn't been the most subtle way of solving things.

'She just thought the plants were dead,' she answered, hoping Katy would go for it. 'They were only a bit wilted really.'

Katy made a disbelieving face, then, as the others headed back towards their table, winked at Sophie and continued, 'Anyway, how was Sunday? Did you catch that Jareth Quinn film?'

'Of course,' Sophie replied. 'I wouldn't have missed it!' She'd decided to be on friendly terms with Katy for as long as the witch hunter was around. Sophie needed a chance to think about her tactics. After all, if Katy discovered Sophie's secret . . . She shuddered. It didn't bear thinking about. Maybe she could convince Katy to give up the hunt. But then she'd be stuck with her all year . . . *This is the most confused I've ever been in my life!*

Katy smiled, oblivious to the thoughts swirling around Sophie's head. 'I loved the scene with the surprise party – so funny! What was your favourite bit?'

Before Sophie could reply, Mrs Stevenson came in, carrying a sheaf of papers.

'OK, class, results time!' she announced. 'Good news first. Erin Best – I am really impressed with your project! You obviously worked very hard to catch up.' She stopped, smiling, in front of Erin's desk and put her folder down on it. Erin squealed with delight and held her project in front of her, the big red A clearly visible on the front. Sophie beamed at her friend.

'Not to mention the fact that your tomatoes are the biggest in the class – and they taste amazing. I couldn't resist trying one this morning.' Mrs Stevenson smiled at Erin and moved on. Sophie couldn't avoid catching Katy's eye. Katy nodded meaningfully, and mouthed a single word: *Witch*.

FOURTEEN

As soon as the lunch bell went, Sophie grabbed her things and rushed out of the lab, hoping to escape Katy. But as she left the Science block she heard footsteps hurrying up behind her, and Katy's voice called out, 'Sophie, wait for me!'

Sophie turned round reluctantly.

'Um, yeah, Jareth Quinn,' she said quickly, hoping to divert Katy's attention from Erin. 'Wasn't he hilarious?'

Katy smiled quickly. 'As always!'

'So what do you think of his new hair?' Sophie went on, but Katy broke in.

'I'm really sorry, Soph, but we've got work to do.' She dropped her voice, pulling Sophie aside from the crowd. 'I'm positive Erin's the witch. And she's getting stronger every day!'

'But the iron filings didn't show anything,' Sophie pointed out, fear plunging through her. If Katy only realised she was talking to the actual witch right now!

'Yes, but remember what I said about the magnet?' Katy stopped speaking as Erin and Lauren walked past them, laughing and chatting about Erin's great project. 'There are other tests we can try, anyway,' she went on, following Erin with her eyes. 'Nothing painful – for now.' She turned back to Sophie. 'Hey, are you OK? You look a bit ill.'

'I – I—' Sophie stumbled. She didn't know what to think. As long as Katy suspected Erin, she wouldn't suspect Sophie. And Erin definitely wasn't a witch – so did it really matter if Katy tested her? But being mixed up in magic was a dangerous game. What if Erin got hurt?

'It's my Art project,' she said, picking the first excuse that came into her head. 'I can't get the collage right, and Art's right after lunch.'

Katy smiled at her warmly.

'I'll help if you like. I'm not great at Art – not like Lauren – but I'd be really glad to help. Especially as you've been so kind, helping me with the witch hunting. No one's ever helped me before.' She slipped her arm through Sophie's as they went up the steps into the main building. 'It's so good to be able to talk to someone who knows the truth. I don't have to pretend any more,' she said, squeezing Sophie's arm as they went through the door.

Sophie forced a smile, although she felt as if her arm was caught in a trap. Her grandmother's words echoed in her mind. *All the Gibsons are very, very dangerous!* She looked around, hoping a friend would turn up and get her away from Katy. But no one did.

'... You don't know how sick I am of all this,' Katy continued as they headed towards the lunch hall. 'I mean, I know what I'm doing is important ... but sometimes I just wish my parents would let me live my own life.'

'They *did* seem a bit on your back,' Sophie couldn't help agreeing.

Katy laughed unhappily. 'They nag me all the time about finding witches. Then as soon as I've found the witch in a school they take me straight out and put me into another school, and I have to start pretending all over again. I hate going through the routine.'

Sophie felt she had to ask: 'What do you mean, *the routine*?'

'Well, when I get to a new school, I pretend to be shy and lonely. That makes people feel sorry for me, and they want to be friends. Works much better than being over-the-top friendly – that just scares people off.'

'Oh ...' Sophie couldn't help feeling hurt, even though she knew why Katy had been pretending.

'Then, when I sniff out some suspects,' Katy continued, her voice sing-song as if she were reciting a recipe, 'I try to get as close to them as possible, to see who's casting spells. I mean, I need to narrow the odds,' she added, reverting to her usual tone. 'I can't just go around chucking handfuls of iron filings at everyone – people might think I was a bit weird!' She made a funny face, and Sophie surprised herself by laughing. For an instant she felt as comfortable as if she was hanging out with a real friend.

Katy laughed too, looking relieved that Sophie got the joke. Then her expression became serious, even a little sad.

'It's so nice to have a friend,' she said quietly. 'Someone I can be honest with ... I've never had that before. Thanks, Sophie. I'm really glad I met you.'

Sophie didn't know what to say. It was impossible not to feel sorry for Katy – in one way she was like everyone else, just wanted people to like her and people to hang out with. But Sophie was a witch, and Katy was a witch hunter. How could they ever be friends?

'You know these other tests,' she said, trying to change the subject. 'What exactly are they? I mean, what do you do?'

'Well, the best way to find out if someone's a witch

is to get hold of their Source,' said Katy. Sophie tried not to glance down at her ring. 'It's the object that channels all their power. That's one reason I'm sure Erin's the witch. Her gold bracelet. She's really protective of it, and it's been passed down in the family – it sounds exactly like a Source.' She frowned. 'What we've got to do is steal the bracelet, melt it down and do a witch hunters' experiment on it. That will tell us if she's a witch – and, if she is, it will destroy her powers, too.'

'S-steal it? But how?'

Katy shrugged as if it was the easiest thing in the world. 'Oh, I'm very good at slipping jewellery off people without them knowing – my parents made me practise lots. Next time Erin's wearing it, I'll get it.'

Sophie's heart sank. She knew Erin would be heartbroken if her bracelet disappeared. There was no way she could let that happen.

'You'll have to wait for ages then,' she said quickly. 'Erin hardly ever wears it at school. It would be quicker if I took it. I know where she keeps it.'

As she spoke, she was thinking fast. She had a

bracelet a lot like Erin's, only not real gold. If she could bring that along, pretending it was Erin's bracelet, Katy could melt it down and Erin's own bracelet wouldn't have to be touched.

'Sophie, that's a brilliant suggestion!' Katy exclaimed. 'What would I do without you?' She glanced at her watch. 'Let's do it now.'

'But ...' Sophie said in horror. 'Wouldn't it be better to wait?'

'No way. Erin's at violin practice. This is the perfect time – she's out of the way.'

Sophie couldn't think of a single excuse. She followed Katy reluctantly in the direction of Erin's dorm.

Sophie gingerly pushed open the door.

'Is the coast clear?' Katy whispered.

'No, young lady, it is not!' snapped a voice behind them. Sophie jumped and Katy gasped. Sophie turned round to see Mrs Freeman scowling at them. She beckoned them away from the door. Sophie and Katy exchanged a despairing look, but they followed her back down the corridor.

'You know perfectly well the dorms are out of bounds in lunch hour,' Mrs Freeman scolded them.

'Oh please, Mrs Freeman, I need to get a book for the next lesson,' Katy began.

'Well, you should have thought of that this morning. School rules are quite clear. Now off you go!'

There was nothing to do but walk away.

'That was bad luck!' Katy exclaimed as soon as Mrs Freeman was out of earshot. 'I'll just have to do it myself after all.'

'No!' Sophie protested. 'Let me try again.'

'But how—'

'I know another way to get in,' Sophie said, off the top of her head.

Katy looked at her, biting her lip. 'Fine. But I've got to have it by the end of the day.'

'The end of the *day*?' Sophie exclaimed.

'Yes! The witch's powers are getting stronger every minute.'

I hope they are, thought Sophie – *at this rate I'm going to need them!*

Katy sighed as they walked away from the dorms.

'Poor Erin. Even if she's a witch, I hate to think how upset she'll be when she finds her bracelet gone.' She raised her head as the bell for the end of lunch hour went. 'Oh, I'd better hurry and collect my portfolio. See you in Art! I promise I'll help with the collage.'

Sophie stared after her in horror as she ran off down the corridor. Her plan was not going to work. If she just substituted one of her own bracelets, Erin wouldn't be upset, and Katy would realise something was up. She was going to actually have to steal her best friend's bracelet in order to save it from the flames, and, what's more, do it by the end of the day. This was harder than Maggie's extra prep!

Fifteen minutes later, Sophie was standing at the side of the girls' dormitory block looking up at the sheer wall. The Year 9 dormitories were on the fourth floor and the window was open. Gally clambered out of her bag and sat on her shoulder, looking up at it with her. His nose twitched doubtfully.

'How on earth am I going to climb this, Gally?' Sophie asked him, stroking his tail. 'It's not as easy as a tree.' She looked around. 'There isn't even a drain-pipe or anything. If only that jasmine had grown further ...' She stared at the jasmine that clustered, thick and green, around the first-floor window. 'Oh wait – that's it!'

Gally jumped back in her bag as she rushed towards her mother's potting shed. Once inside, she scooped up a big handful of fertiliser and ran back to the jasmine. She knelt down and put the fertiliser on to the ground where the roots were. She touched it with her ring, hoping this would make it more effective.

'Earth, water, wind and fire,' she whispered, work-ing it in with her fingers, 'Forces of the Earth, make this jasmine grow as high as the roof!'

She flinched back as the stem of the jasmine expanded before her eyes. Like a green balloon inflat-ing, it zoomed up the walls, spreading its twigs like fingers and digging into the mortar, until its topmost leaves waved in the wind at the roof. Sophie looked up at it, open-mouthed. She hadn't expected it to grow so much faster than the tomato plant.

'Amazing!' she breathed with a grin. She looked at

her ring, impressed. Katy was right, her powers were getting stronger. 'Witches must have a connection to nature. Maybe that's why I've always had green fingers.'

She dropped her bag. 'Come on, Gally!'

Gally scampered across the ground and ran up the jasmine. He paused at the first-floor window, looking down as if to encourage her. Sophie took a deep breath and began to climb.

Several minutes later she was hanging high above the ground, level with the third-floor window. Her fingers were aching and she was panting for breath. She felt for a toe-hold, her foot slipping before she could wedge it into a cleft in the vines. A strand of jasmine blew into her face, so she couldn't see where she was going. With a desperate heave and a scramble, she pulled herself up another few inches. Gally looked down at her anxiously.

'Just a minute, Gally. I've got to rest . . .'

The third-floor window was just above her, and it was open. She pulled herself up, tearing small leaves as she struggled for a hand-hold, grabbed the ledge and leaned her elbows on it. She had barely got her breath when through the window she saw Mrs Freeman at the far end of the corridor. And she was walking towards her.

'Uh-oh!' Sophie hastily put on a burst of speed and scrambled upwards as fast as she could. She steadied herself above the window, one foot resting on the top of the frame. Glancing down, she saw Mrs Freeman's arm come out, grab the handle of the window and pull it closed with a bang. Sophie nearly screamed as her foot slipped into thin air. For a horrible moment she was dangling by her hands; then her foot jammed into a tangle of branches and she steadied herself.

Sophie breathed out, her heart hammering. She looked up. Gally was at the fourth-floor window, leaning down to watch her. The window was open.

'OK, Gally, I'm coming,' she called, her voice shaking, and began climbing again. Finally, she reached it, and with a huge effort heaved herself over the windowsill. She toppled on to the floor and lay there, catching her breath and resting her aching arms.

Gally peered into her face, making her laugh.

'All right, I get the message – no time for lying

down!' She got to her feet and went over to Erin's bed. Erin had said she kept the bracelet in her top drawer, which was locked – but everyone knew she kept the key behind her dressing table mirror. Sophie felt for the key and unlocked the drawer. Inside lay the shining gold bracelet.

Sophie took a deep breath. Reaching out and taking the bracelet felt harder than climbing the wall, but there was nothing else she could do.

As she picked it up, a piece of notepaper came out of the drawer along with it. She bent down to pick it up. She didn't mean to read it, but Erin's big loopy handwriting in pink pen was hard to miss. The paper was headed: *To-Do List for Sophie's Surprise Party!!* Underneath, she recognised all her friends' handwriting. Joanna had written *Ask Mum to send cookies.* Lauren had added *Make cake!!* Erin had noted *Buy balloons,* and Kaz had added *Tell Callum!*

Sophie's mouth fell open. She clutched the list tight. She realised how much she'd been worrying that her friends didn't like her any more, now that they had Katy. She looked from the list to the bracelet. Now it seemed even more impossible to walk away with Erin's favourite possession.

But she had to.

Sophie placed the list back in the drawer and slipped the bracelet into her pocket.

'I'm so sorry, Erin,' she whispered as she put the key back.

*

As Sophie left the main building after the end of lessons with everyone else, she saw Katy waving to her from under the old oak tree. Reluctantly, she went over and sat down next to her on the grass. She watched Callum walking over to the library. She wanted to call out to him, but what was the point in involving him in this mess? *The fewer people who know, the better*, she told herself. She'd never thought anything would get between herself and her best friend.

'So, how did it go?' Katy began. 'Did you get it?'

Before Sophie could reply, she heard someone calling her name. She turned round to see Erin racing towards them, in floods of tears.

'Sophie! Katy! Oh my god – I can't believe it!'

Katy flashed a knowing look at Sophie, then jumped to her feet and caught Erin as she reached them.

'Erin – what's the matter?' she demanded.

'It's my bracelet – it's gone! Someone's stolen it!' Erin buried her face in Katy's shoulder and sobbed.

'Oh no!' Katy exclaimed. She gave Sophie a thumbs up behind Erin's back. Sophie couldn't bring herself to smile.

'It was in my bedside drawer, and now it's gone,' came Erin's muffled voice. She raised her head. Her face was puffy and pink with crying.

Sophie turned pale. 'I'm so sorry!' she gasped.

Katy cast her a warning glance and said hastily, 'Are you sure you left it in your drawer? Couldn't you have lost it somewhere – dropped it, perhaps?'

Erin shook her head hard. 'No way. I'm so careful with it. Someone has been in my drawer and stolen it. There's a thief in this school – I'm going to tell a prefect!' She looked up as Maggie walked past. 'Maggie! Maggie!'

Maggie hurried over.

'Maggie, someone in this school is a thief!' Erin burst out as she reached them.

Maggie's eyes widened with delight and she whipped out a little red notebook and a pen.

'Tell me everything!' she commanded.

Maggie listened, making notes and now and then snorting indignantly, as Erin told her story. Sophie and Katy exchanged nervous glances.

'I can't believe someone would have done this to me,' Erin finished, blinking back tears.

Maggie closed her notebook with a snap and wagged her finger at Erin. 'Well, it was very irresponsible of you to keep a valuable object in your room. You should have handed it to Mrs Freeman for safekeeping.' Erin began to sniff again, and Katy rolled her eyes at Sophie. 'But that's no excuse for theft, of course. Leave this with me, Erin. I shall make it my mission to catch the thief and get your bracelet back.'

'Oh, thank you, Maggie,' Erin exclaimed.

'No need to thank me. This is the kind of thing the office of Head Prefect was created for.' Maggie turned away, but spun on her heel to add, 'And when I do catch them, they'll definitely be expelled. Turlingham has a zero-tolerance policy on theft!'

Sophie gulped as Maggie strode away.

Erin sighed. 'She's not so bad after all, I guess.' She took the tissue Katy offered her and blew her nose. 'I just can't believe it,' she said sadly. 'Who would be so mean as to take my bracelet? I thought I could trust everyone at Turlingham.' She began to sob again, and Sophie put a hand on her arm wordlessly. She had never felt so awful in her life – but she had to see her plan through. It was the only way to save Erin's bracelet for real!

With a quick glance to check no one was crossing the moonlit courtyard, Sophie pushed open the door of the Science block and slipped inside. *Strange how this sneaking around is beginning to feel normal,* she thought as she headed up the corridor to where light shone out of the Chemistry lab. Before Katy had come to the school, Sophie had thought of herself as a pretty good pupil – well, there had been that thing with the

water balloons, but that had been Kaz's idea, really –
but now she wondered if there was a single school rule
left she hadn't broken. Her mother didn't know the
half of it. Poor Mum – Sophie had kept quiet ever
since their visit to Grandma. Whenever her mum
tried to ask if she was OK, Sophie closed up. What was
the point in loading her mum with a whole ton of
secrets?

She found Katy in the Chemistry lab, wearing her
white coat and protective goggles. In front of her was
a china dish above a Bunsen burner, a whole row of
test tubes, and different jars of powder and liquid.
Some of them Sophie recognised, like the sulphuric
acid and the magnesium, but others were very strange –
there was a shimmery rainbow powder that seemed
to crawl around the dish as if it were alive, different
shades of purple liquids, and a jar of some powder
that was a colour she had never seen before.

Katy smiled as she turned to Sophie, but her smile
quickly disappeared. Sophie noticed she had bags
under her eyes, as if she hadn't slept well.

'So – let's see this bracelet,' Katy said.

Sophie took a deep breath, reached in her pocket and pulled it out. Not Erin's bracelet. She had left that one in her bag, and instead had brought her own. It was gold coloured and it was a similar size to Erin's, but it didn't have the pearl set into it that Erin's bracelet had. She watched nervously as Katy took it. If she noticed, the game was up. But Katy just glanced at the bracelet and placed it in the dish.

'Well done!' she said with a half smile. 'You've got talent – you could be a witch hunter yourself.'

I doubt it, Sophie thought, but she smiled back. Katy picked up a pipette, turned to the test tubes and began adding one of the purple liquids to the dish. A drop splashed on to her hand.

'Ouch!' She snatched her hand to her mouth and turned away quickly – but not before Sophie had glimpsed tears in her eyes.

'Are you OK?' Sophie asked.

Katy nodded. 'I'm sorry. I'm just ... distracted.' Her mouth twisted sadly as she continued adding liquid to the china dish. 'I guess I feel bad about Erin.'

'You mean you don't think she's a witch after all?' Sophie exclaimed, her heart leaping.

'Oh no – she's a witch, all right.' Katy shrugged and put the pipette down. As she unscrewed the lid of a jar of shimmery powder, she added, 'So I know it's wrong to feel sorry for her. You must think I'm weak.'

Sophie opened her mouth to deny it, but Katy went on, almost as if she was talking to herself.

'I'm sure – well, as sure as I can be – that under her sweet exterior she's really an evil witch, and the reason she's so upset is because she's lost her Source. But . . . it was still horrible to see her cry.' She fell silent, and added a teaspoon of the shimmery powder to the mixture in the china dish. The powder went in with a quick hiss. 'I guess it just shows how easy it is for a witch to worm her way into your heart.' As she said the word *witch*, the mixture in the dish spat black sparks. Sophie jumped, glad she'd left Gally behind. He'd be freaking out by now!

Katy pulled on her protective goggles.

'I suppose I'd better get on with it,' she said without enthusiasm. To Sophie, she added, 'Keep well back, because this can be dangerous. A mixture just like this once exploded on my mother.'

Sophie remembered the scar on Mrs Gibson's face. So the Gibson parents did experiments like this too. She peered over Katy's shoulder as she began to chant and make circles with her hand over the dish. It shot through her mind that, even though the bracelet wasn't her Source, it still might betray her in some way. What if witches left magical fingerprints that would show up in a test like this? Or perhaps – her heart sank – Katy was bluffing. Maybe she knew perfectly well that Sophie was a witch, and she was playing some sort of game so she could trap her properly. After all, hadn't she said that witch hunters had to pretend to be friends with their enemies in order to catch them out?

'Katy,' she said, hesitating as she tried to get the words just right, 'Erin's nice, isn't she? You like her, right?'

'I said I did, didn't I?' Katy turned up the heat on the Bunsen burner and the mixture seethed and bubbled.

'But then . . . do you have to do this? I mean, even if she's a witch.' Sophie moved closer, trying to see Katy's face behind the goggles. 'Couldn't you just . . . couldn't we just . . . leave her alone?'

Katy's eyebrows raised above the goggles, though she didn't glance up from the dish.

'Nice isn't the same as good, Sophie,' she said firmly. 'Witches are evil. They have to have their powers taken away from them, or they have to be – well, killed.' She straightened up and added a last sprinkle of shimmery powder to the mixture. Then she turned to Sophie, and Sophie saw her frowning beneath the goggles. 'It's the only way to keep the rest of the world safe. And I'd rather take Erin's powers away than kill her.'

She began chanting again.

I'm sure I'm not evil, Sophie thought. *I haven't done anything bad – well, I've broken a lot of school rules, but that's not exactly evil. And Grandma didn't seem evil either.*

The things Katy said – they didn't even sound like her own thoughts. They sounded like ideas someone else had put in her head. Yet Katy was clearly convinced she was right.

Katy poured sulphuric acid on to the mixture as she chanted. Sophie couldn't make out what she was saying: there was some French in there, and some Latin, and lots of other strange-sounding words. Green fire danced above the dish.

'Isn't it possible there could be some good witches?' Sophie dared to say.

'No,' said Katy. She clicked her fingers above the dish and the green flames twisted into a spiral.

'So they're *all* evil?'

'Yes.'

'But—'

'Sorry, Soph, I know more about this than you do. Now I really have to concentrate on this.' Katy took a strip of magnesium in the tongs and carefully dropped it into the mixture. The mixture fizzed and sparked, and Sophie edged away. Nothing happened, so she edged forwards again.

'How will you know it's worked?' she said as soon as Katy paused in her chanting. The next second she ducked as a foot-long white flame shot out of the mixture. A loud, angry howling sound, like a pack of wolves, came from the dish, and Katy hastily started chanting again, at the top of her voice.

'*Umbra aut luce, die aut nocte, veritas pateat.*'

Her voice rose to a crescendo, her forehead furrowed in concentration and sweat rolled down her face. Sophie held her breath. The howling died away into silence and the mixture lay still, occasionally blowing a bubble. Sophie peeked into the dish. Her bracelet was a bracelet no more – just a melted pool of metal.

Katy lowered her hands and fell silent. Her head drooped, and to Sophie's astonishment she realised she was crying. Tears streamed down her nose and plopped onto the bench.

'She's *not* a witch,' Katy said between her sobs. 'The bracelet shouldn't just melt like that. I was so sure! And now I've ruined her prized possession – and I've spied on her – and – oh, I hate myself!' She sat down on the floor and sobbed harder. 'I always find the witch, always! But now I've made such a terrible mistake ... I'm supposed to keep ringing my parents to tell them what I've found out, but this time I just don't know, I haven't got a clue. They're going to be so disappointed and cross. I don't want to phone them ... I don't dare!'

Sophie watched her in shock. *How horrible to have parents like that,* she thought. A wave of pity and sympathy for Katy swept over her. She'd been worrying about Katy stealing her friends, but now she realised that Katy was the loneliest girl she'd ever met. She squatted down next to her and gently put an arm round her shoulder.

'And the worst thing is,' Katy wept, 'I really like Erin. I really like all of you. I can't bear to think of how upset Erin is – and it's all my fault. If she knew what I'd done, she'd never speak to me again ... and I wouldn't blame her.'

She sniffed and wiped her sleeve across her eyes.

'I can't fix things,' she said. 'But I'm going to use my pocket money to buy Erin a new bracelet. I don't care how long it takes me to save up – I can do that, at least.'

Sophie looked hard at Katy. There wasn't a single

bit of fakery in Katy's eyes – just unhappiness and regret.

Who was evil? Witches or witch hunters? Sophie needed some answers. And she knew just the person who might have them.

FIFTEEN

The moon shone down as Sophie pulled her bike up outside the gates of the Bowden Psychiatric Hospital. She glanced at her watch.

'Past midnight, Gally,' she whispered to the squirrel, who was perched on the handlebars. 'I hope the nurses are sleeping on the job.'

Gally scampered on to her shoulder as she hid the bike in a hedge. Sophie glanced left and right to check she hadn't been followed, then hurried in through the gates, keeping to the shadows cast by the big chestnut trees. She tiptoed up to the building. It was dark and seemed deserted but Sophie knew that there would be nurses on the night shift. Thinking it would be better to knock on her grandmother's window rather than try to get in through the main doors, she edged her way along the outer wall, peering through the different windows and trying to work out which one might belong to her grandmother. She rounded the corner – and came face to face with a man in a white uniform.

They both gasped at the same moment. The nurse stared at her in shock.

'Hey – what are you doing here?' he shouted.

Sophie searched her mind for a good explanation. Realising there wasn't one, she turned and ran.

The man was running after her. 'Wait!' he shouted.

Sophie raced down the path and swung around the corner of the building, Gally darting ahead of her. Behind, she could hear the man's footsteps, catching up fast. Thinking quick, she darted into the shadow of a tree and grasped its trunk. 'Earth, water, wind and fire – hide me, please!' she whispered.

The tree's shadow seemed to grow darker. Sophie's

ring glowed, and she looked up to see a huge cloud move across the moon. A second later, the nurse ran past her, just an outline in the sudden, deep darkness.

Sophie caught her breath. Her powers had saved her once again. She stepped out on to the path, a little breathless at the thought that her magic had moved an entire cloud. It wouldn't be long before the nurse came back, so she hurried around the building, and saw that one window was standing open. On the sill sat a black raven.

'Look, Gally, it's Corvis!' she whispered. She ran to the window and, sure enough, her grandmother was there, smiling. She opened the window wide and helped Sophie climb over the sill. Corvis flapped into the room after her. Grandma shut the window and drew the curtains.

'I thought it had to be you, when I saw that mysterious cloud pass over the moon,' she said with a smile. 'Sit down there, dear. Cup of tea? And I know your familiar world like a nice bowl of milk.'

Sophie sat down in an armchair and watched her grandmother busy herself in the kitchen area. She still didn't feel quite safe here – she remembered how strange her grandmother had been last time they met, although the old woman didn't acknowledge that now. But as she watched Gally and the raven sitting together like old friends, she relaxed a little. If Gally liked it here, it had to be OK. She didn't know what she was going to tell her grandmother but as the old woman came over and handed her the cup of tea, she looked up into her eyes and blurted out, 'Grandma, I've made a decision.'

Her grandmother stirred her tea. 'Really, dear?'

'Yes,' Sophie said with a quick nod. 'It's about Katy Gibson. I like her, Grandma. I – I want to be her friend.'

A look of shock and pain flickered across her grandmother's face. She sat down slowly and placed her hand on Sophie's.

'Sophie, you have a kind and open heart. But you absolutely mustn't trust Katy Gibson.'

'But Grandma—'

'Let me finish! You see, witch hunters think we are evil, but it's they who are the evil ones.'

'Maybe there are some evil ones, but maybe there are some good ones too,' Sophie protested. 'Maybe the Gibsons will understand when we explain we're not the bad guys! Grandma, did you ever try talking to them?'

Her grandmother shook her head. 'You're the one who doesn't understand, Sophie. The witch community knows all about the Gibsons already.'

Sophie opened her mouth to say, *What witch community*? But her grandmother continued.

'The Gibsons are the worst of them all – the most evil and persistent witch hunters alive.' Her voice fell. 'Sophie . . . it was the Gibsons who drove your father to disappear.'

Sophie froze.

'No,' she whispered.

'I'm sorry you had to find out like this. Sophie, please, wait. Sophie!'

But Sophie was already on her feet. Ignoring her grandmother's pleas, she pushed open the window and scrambled over the sill.

'Sophie! Come back!'

But she didn't turn back. She dropped to the ground and raced towards her bike, Gally at her heels. She pulled the bike out of the hedge and leaned on the handlebars, her head spinning with the horrible knowledge that Katy Gibson – the girl she'd trusted and tried to help – was mixed up in her father's disappearance. Had the Gibsons destroyed his Source and driven him mad? Or had they done something worse . . . Had they killed him?

She jumped on to her bike and rode off, pedalling as fast as she could, desperate to get back to her safe, normal bedroom.

The sun was rising as Sophie slipped out of her house the next morning. She hadn't been able to sleep all night. The sea wind whipped her hair as she ran across the courtyard towards the girls' dormitories, her school bag bumping on her back.

'Hope you're OK in there, Gally,' she whispered. She was trembling, not just because of the chilly air, but because she had decided what to do. She had to know the truth about her father. She was going to demand answers from Katy Gibson. Even if it meant telling her that she was a witch.

As Sophie marched up the stairs of the dormitory block, Maggie came out of the Year 11 bathroom, wearing a dressing gown and with a towel wrapped around her hair. She stared at Sophie in shock.

'What are you doing here?' She blocked her way.

'I don't have time to explain, Maggie,' said Sophie, trembling with nerves. 'Please get out of my way.'

'Oh really?' Maggie said indignantly. 'Prefects have the authority to stop girls who are out of bounds – and you're out of bounds right now. Day girls aren't allowed in dorms before breakfast, not even if they're the headmistress's daughter. You get out or I'll call Mrs Freeman!'

Sophie tried to barge past her. Maggie, taken by surprise, was pushed out of the way. But, as she turned, she grabbed Sophie's bag and pulled it off her back. Sophie spun round halfway up the flight of stairs as she remembered that it wasn't just Gally in her bag – Erin's bracelet was in there, too.

'Please give that back,' she said quietly.

Maggie smirked and dangled the bag teasingly.

'Don't you know what it's like to want to be with friends?' Sophie pleaded. She noticed the Head Prefect's smile falter. 'It's just, Mum and I have had a really tough week with family things and ... ' She paused and saw a shadow of hesitation pass over Maggie's face. 'That's the only reason I'm here. I just wanted to slip in and see my friends before school began because we can't talk properly in class. Is that so difficult to understand?'

Maggie's hand, holding the bag, started to lower.

'Go on, then,' she said, her voice thick with emotion. 'Take your bag. I'll pretend I never saw you – just this once!' She spat the last words, some of her old energy returning.

'Thank you, Maggie!' Sophie gushed. The Head Prefect had no idea there was a stolen bracelet and a squirrel in the bag! She ducked down to retrieve it and Maggie turned on her heel, striding away. Sophie never thought she'd say it, but she was grateful to the older girl.

She turned to go up the stairs, but there was a

squeak and Gally leapt out of the bag, racing up the stairs before her.

'Get back here!' Sophie cried, looking round to check no one saw, then racing after her familiar. Once she got there she found the Year 9 dorm in uproar, with girls in pyjamas running around shrieking, 'The squirrel! Did you see it? It came right in here!'

Sophie made her way to Erin's bed. Erin and Lauren were standing on Erin's bed while Kaz was on her hands and knees, peering under the furniture. Erin spotted Sophie and squealed, 'Sophie! Oh my god! There was a black squirrel in here – it ran in from the corridor and went under the beds!'

'Erin, I'm sorry, but I've got to talk to Katy, right now,' said Sophie, no longer able to worry about what Gally was up to. 'Do you guys know where she is?'

'Her phone rang and she went out. Why? What do you want to speak to her about?' Lauren asked.

'Sorry – I can't . . . ' Sophie turned and raced out of the room. She ran to the bathroom at the far end of the dormitory and pushed it open, but Katy was nowhere to be seen. She rushed to the stairs and looked out of the landing windows. There was a figure crossing towards the light house. Katy. She ran down and banged out of the doors.

'Katy!' she yelled as she ran across the courtyard.

Katy turned as she approached, but, instead of waiting for her, she sped up, running for the gap in the fence to get to the meadow.

Sophie ran after her. 'Katy! I need to talk to you!' she shouted, but Katy didn't pause.

Sophie caught up with her just as she ducked under the gap in the fence. She followed her through, grabbed her arm and spun her round.

'There's something I need to say,' she gasped.

'Now isn't a good time.' Katy pulled free. Sophie followed, determined she wouldn't escape.

'It's important!'

Katy backed away. She was trembling, her eyes darting around as if she expected to be attacked.

'Sophie – you have to hide. In there. In the lighthouse, quick.' She pushed her towards the door. Sophie resisted, but when she caught Katy's glance again, she was suddenly frightened. She'd never seen Katy look so afraid.

'OK – but then we need to talk,' she said fiercely.

She shouldered the door open and stepped inside, pushing it closed behind her. There was a bright crack of light in the old wood, and she put her eye to it and watched as Katy turned on the spot, shivering, her fists clenched as if she were ready to fight a monster.

But it wasn't a monster that came round the side of the lighthouse. It was Ashton.

SIXTEEN

As she peered through the crack, Sophie saw that Ashton's face was twisted in an angry frown. Suddenly, he looked less handsome than he did before.

She shifted to get a better view. Ashton grabbed Katy's arm and it made Sophie jump in shock. Katy let out a gasp and Sophie saw a look of pain cross her face. Her heart turned to ice. So it was Ashton that Katy was so afraid of.

He pulled Katy right up to the wall of the lighthouse.

Sophie was so close that she could see the muscle twitching in his jaw.

'Did you bring anyone else?' he began in an angry whisper. 'You'd better not have.'

'N–no, Ashton, I promise I didn't.' Katy sounded terrified.

'Good.' He pushed her away. 'I don't like the way you've been sucking up to your new mates here. Getting a bit too friendly, I reckon.'

'I have to. You know I have to!'

'We're not here to have fun. We're here to find a witch. And you'd better hurry up: I've already ruled out all the boys and I'm getting bored of being stuck here on top of this dumb-ass cliff with this bunch of losers.' He glanced around as if looking to see if they were being watched. Sophie held her breath, but he didn't look towards the lighthouse door. 'I think you need something to concentrate your mind on the job. So here's the deal: if you haven't found the witch by Friday, I'm going to make sure you're the laughing stock of the Welcome Back Dance.'

Sophie pulled back, feeling as if she had been

punched in the stomach. The way his lip curled and his brow creased in a frown – this wasn't the smiling boy she'd spoken to only a few days ago.

Katy laughed disbelievingly. 'How are you going to do that?'

Ashton grinned and pulled a book out of his bag. It was pink and black with ragged edges of paper sticking out of it, and doodles across the front.

'My diary!' Katy cried. She tried to snatch it but Ashton easily moved out of the way. He opened the pages and started reading.

'*Day One at Turlingham and I'm sick of lying already.*' Ashton was putting on a high-pitched voice as he spoke, mocking Katy. '*This is a photo of the girls I met today.*' He held up the book and Sophie's eyes widened as she saw it was a photo that Katy had snapped in the lunch hall the day she'd arrived. '*I pretended I liked them, as usual, same old blah blah blah. I give this dump a week at most.* I'm sure your so-called friends are going to love finding out exactly how two-faced you are.'

'Give it back!' Katy cried out.

'Are you kidding? I haven't got to the juiciest bit yet.' Ashton flicked through the pages. 'Oh, look – here's a photo of you sucking up to the headmistress's daughter.' He turned the book round and Sophie felt sick as she saw it was a photo of her and Katy hugging. Her own smile looked distinctly fake in that photo, she realised. 'Ooh, this bit needs violins. *I feel like Sophie's my best friend, like she really understands me. I've never had a friend like this before, someone I can trust. I think Callum must be really nice, because he's friends with her too. I really, really like him* . . . Aw, how cute,' he sneered. 'And you've drawn a picture of him all covered with hearts. How touching. And oh – what's this?' He held up the book and Sophie could see something small and silver taped on to the page. '*I dropped this 5p coin in the hallway today and he picked it up for me. I'm keeping it because his hand actually touched it.*' Ashton burst into laughter. 'This is going to go down a storm when I read it out at the dance!'

Katy turned white. 'Ashton, no!' She lunged desperately for the book. 'Please, please, give it back – I'd die if Callum found out how I felt about him!'

'Oh, come on, it would be worse if he found out how you *used* to feel about him,' said Ashton, ducking out of her way. 'Hmm, now where's the good bit . . . oh yes, here we are. Not so many hearts here, huh?'

He turned the book round so Katy could see it. Pressing her face to the door, Sophie cringed as she saw a sketch of Callum – with greasy hair and glasses. Next to the sketch, Katy had written: *Class A geek – major loser!*

Katy's shoulders shook and she pressed her hands to her face.

'Please,' she sobbed, 'please don't show him that. It's not fair. I didn't know him then. Please, Ashton. I really, really like him.'

Ashton clapped the diary shut and shoved it back in his bag.

'You'd better hurry up and catch this witch then, hadn't you, sis?' he said. 'Because if you haven't caught her by Friday, I'm going to bring this book to the dance, and Callum and everyone else will see exactly what you think of them.'

'But I can't *find* the witch!' Katy shouted, on the

217

edge of tears. 'I can't find her this time – I've tried, I've tried my hardest!'

Ashton shrugged. 'That's your problem, not mine,' he said. 'Mum and Dad are going to be so disappointed in you.' He turned and walked away, whistling.

As soon as she was sure he had gone, Sophie opened the door. Katy was sitting on the floor. She wasn't crying – but the look on her face made Sophie's heart break.

Sophie crouched down and put her arms round her. Katy's shoulders trembled as she burst into tears.

'I don't know what to do,' Katy sobbed into her shoulder. 'I hate that my parents use me for witch hunting – but how can I let them down? They're my *parents*! And if Ashton shows that book to everyone, I think I'll die. I couldn't bear it. I've been so two-faced . . . but . . . ' She sniffed. 'I was telling the truth when I wrote you were my best friend, Sophie. I promise. Cross my heart.'

Sophie stroked Katy's hair, deep in thought. Everything had changed, she realised. Whatever Katy's parents might have done to her father, it wasn't Katy's fault. Her grandmother's warnings rang in Sophie's ears, but she realised that she couldn't listen. *This isn't about witches or witch hunters,* she thought. *It's about friends.* She had to help Katy. She had to really be her friend.

SEVENTEEN

It was Friday – the day of the dance.

Sophie pushed open the big double doors of the school hall. A wave of party music, laughter and excited conversation rolled towards her; some people were already on the dance floor. Girls and boys milled around each other in tight crowds, chattering excitedly and flirting. They didn't have to wear uniform for once and there were so many colours swirling around that Sophie felt like she was standing inside a kaleidoscope! Sophie scanned the room anxiously, wondering if

Ashton had realised that she'd stood him up. She turned to Katy, who had followed her in, and shouted over the music, 'I can't see him anywhere. Maybe he's changed his mind?'

Katy shook her head. 'Ashton's not like that,' she said. 'He's just waiting for the perfect moment to humiliate me.' In a lower voice, she added, 'If only I'd found the witch, this wouldn't have happened.'

Sophie's heart skipped a beat, but she answered quickly, 'Don't blame yourself. Ashton's a bully, that's all.' She cringed inside to think how pleased she'd been when he'd asked her to the dance. There was no way she'd ever date him now that she knew what he was really like.

There were plenty of boys in the room, tall sixth-formers lounging by the wall, and tiny Year 7s running around noisily, but Ashton was nowhere to be seen. Sophie turned her attention to the dance floor – and grabbed Katy's arm in excitement.

'Oh, look! Erin and Mark are dancing together!'

'Where?' Katy looked eagerly. 'Aw, that's so sweet!'

Erin, in a gold sequinned top and skinny jeans, was

dancing shyly with Mark. Sophie noticed that for once he wasn't checking his reflection every two minutes. Instead he was gazing at Erin with a lovestruck expression on his face.

'I guess he really did like her after all,' said Katy, with a smile.

Sophie smiled back. She couldn't tell Katy, but the nicest thing was that she knew Mark liking Erin wasn't down to magic – this was real. Sophie hadn't done any more spells to make this happen.

'Let's go over and say hi,' she suggested. They made their way through the crowd. Sophie tapped Erin on the shoulder.

'Hey, party girl – love your outfit!' she said with a grin as Erin turned round.

'Sophie, oh my god, you look amazing!' Erin exclaimed. 'And Katy, that green silk is too cute. It totally makes your eyes zing.'

'Enjoying the party?' Sophie asked, glancing at Mark meaningfully.

Erin grinned back at her, blushing. 'Loving it!'

'Guess we'll leave you to it then!' Sophie said. She

was about to move away so they could be alone, when Katy put out a hand to stop her. She had a strange, stunned expression on her face. Sophie looked at her questioningly and followed her gaze. Her stomach flip-flopped as she saw what Katy was looking at.

'Erin ... nice bracelet,' said Katy. She took Erin's wrist and lifted it up. The gold flashed and the pearl winked in the disco lights.

Erin looked embarrassed. 'Oh yeah ... I didn't tell you but I found it under my bed when the squirrel ran under there.'

Sophie smiled to herself as she thought of her familiar – when she'd realised that Gally had returned Erin's bracelet she could've kissed him!

'So no one took it?' Katy asked, turning the bracelet over and over, examining it closely with a frown on her face.

'No. I feel really dumb for making such a fuss.'

'Um. We should go.' Sophie tried to drag Katy away. 'Catch you later, Erin!' She hoped her voice wasn't shaking too much.

As they walked, Katy whispered in Sophie's ear, 'When did you get the replacement bracelet?'

Sophie put on a burst of speed, pretending not to hear her over the music.

Katy hurried after her. 'The one we melted was plain,' she continued. 'This one has a pearl set into it. I don't get it. She can't honestly believe it's her old bracelet – can she?' She caught Sophie's arm and pulled her round to face her. 'Sophie, what's going on?'

Sophie felt herself turn hot and red. She opened her mouth desperately.

'I – I —'

'Um – excuse me . . .' Callum's voice broke in.

Sophie turned round in surprise. Callum was standing behind her, shifting from foot to foot. His hair was unnaturally tidy, and he was wearing a smart shirt and a nervous expression.

'Oh, hi, Callum,' she began. Then she realised Callum wasn't looking at her, but at Katy.

'Um,' he began, 'I wondered if you'd, er, like to, er, dance? With me, I mean. Obviously. Er—'

'Yes!' Katy interrupted him, turning bright pink.

She cast Sophie a thrilled glance as Callum took her hand and led her towards the dance floor. Sophie's astonishment turned to delight as she watched them shyly begin to dance with each other. She realised there was no one she'd rather see Callum end up with than Katy. It was perfect, her two best friends getting together ...

Is that what Katy is, then? Sophie realised. *My new best friend?*

But she was also her most dangerous enemy!

As she thought that, her smile died. At the same moment, the music faded out and the main lights were switched on. Sophie looked up to see Mrs Freeman on the stage, holding a microphone.

'Is this thing on?' she said, looking at it as if it were a snake about to strangle her. 'Oh, it is. Oh – ah – very well.' She cleared her throat. 'Boys and girls, students of Turlingham! I hope you are enjoying yourselves. I won't keep you long with this little welcome speech—'

Sophie heard the doors at the back of the hall open and swing closed. She turned and saw that Ashton had just entered. He had something square and bulky under his jacket. As she watched, he sidled over to the edge of the hall and disappeared into the crowd.

Sophie spun round and began pushing her way through the crowd towards Katy.

'Excuse me – sorry—'

Reaching Katy, she tapped her shoulder and whispered, 'He's here.'

Katy's face fell and she dropped Callum's hand. Sophie scanned the crowd and pointed Ashton out. He was at the far side of the hall, making his way up towards the stage. Sophie and Katy exchanged a glance, and, without another word, headed towards him as fast as they could, ignoring Callum's confused expression.

Ashton turned as they caught up with him.

'There you are!' he exclaimed, looking at Sophie with a sneering expression. 'I can't believe your nerve. You must be crazy to stand me up!'

Katy glanced at Sophie, looking taken aback.

'You had a date with Ashton?'

'Yeah, incredibly I lowered my standards enough to

ask her to the dance,' Ashton snapped. Sophie felt her face flush with anger, but kept calm as he looked at her. 'You'll never get another chance like that again, loser.' He turned to Katy. 'As for you . . . ' He tapped the bulky object under his jacket. 'Have you done what you were supposed to?'

'No,' Katy said, her voice trembling. 'But I tried . . . really hard. It's not my fault I can't this time. Ashton, please!' she begged, as Ashton pulled the diary out from under his jacket and dangled it teasingly out of reach. 'I've got it under control, I promise. I just need a bit more time. Mum and Dad don't need to know.'

'Too late, already told them,' Ashton said, casually tossing the diary in the air. Sophie snatched for it but he whisked it away. 'They'll be here soon – and you'll be in soooo much trouble.'

Without warning, he barged past them and dashed for the stage. Sophie tried to grab him but he shoved her aside, hard, knocking her into a group of Year 10 girls, who screamed as their soft drinks spilled.

'Sorry, I'm so sorry.' Sophie picked herself up and

chased after Ashton. Ashton cut through the crowd, knocking people out of his way and leaving a trail of angry pupils. Katy and Sophie struggled after him. Ashton swerved to the right, heading for a small door marked No Entry.

'Oh, Sophie, that's the stage door!' Katy gasped. 'We've got to stop him!'

Sophie found herself mouthing *Earth, water, wind and fire* – but she stopped herself saying it aloud. How could she use magic when there was a witch hunter right next to her? Instead, she ran as fast as she could, reaching the door just after Ashton. He slammed it in her face, but she yanked it open. Inside, there were stairs leading up to the stage. She and Katy rushed up them and found themselves faced with a barrier of red velvet curtain. As Sophie desperately looked for a way through, she heard the hall fall silent. Katy, who was just behind her, grabbed her arm. 'Oh no, he's going to do it!'

'Yes, Ashton?' Sophie heard Mrs Freeman say.

'I'm sorry to interrupt you, Mrs Freeman,' she heard Ashton reply smoothly, speaking loudly for the benefit of the crowd. 'My sister really wanted to make a speech, but she's too shy. So I wondered if I could read it out for her. It's all about, you know, being new at Turlingham, and her first impressions.'

Sophie finally found a gap in the curtains and pulled them aside. Ashton was at the microphone and he had the diary open at the page with Callum's caricature on it. Behind her, she heard Katy whimper.

Sophie took a deep breath. She couldn't use magic herself – but maybe Gally could help. She glanced up at the ceiling, where Gally had been hiding himself in among the ropes and the walkways. His bright, intelligent eyes met her own.

'Go for it, Gally!' Sophie mouthed silently from her hidden place in the wings.

With one flying leap, Gally was scuttling along a rope and down the curtains.

'Like this, for example.' Ashton held up the diary to show the caricature to the whole school – but, as he did so, a dark shape dropped from above and landed on the book, knocking it out of his hands. The students in the first row squealed, then burst into laughter and shouts of 'It's a squirrel!', as Gally grabbed the diary and dashed into the wings with it. He reached Sophie and sat up on his hind legs, his nose quivering as he nudged the diary towards her.

Sophie dropped to her knees and gently took it.

'Thanks, Gally,' she whispered.

She straightened up and offered the book to Katy. Katy's hands closed on it automatically. But, instead of thanking her, she gazed at Sophie with a look of horror and disbelief.

'That squirrel is your familiar,' Katy gasped. 'It's you. You're the witch!'

EIGHTEEN

The next moment the curtain was pushed aside in a flurry of red velvet and Ashton stormed up to them. Sophie could hear a teacher making a hurried announcement into the microphone and then music starting up again. Katy backed away, to the top of the stairs, holding her diary tight against her chest. Sophie couldn't help taking a step back too.

Ashton stabbed a finger at Katy. 'You did this,' he hissed. 'You put the squirrel up to it! You're no better than a witch – using your powers for evil!'

He grabbed the diary and tried to wrench it out of her grasp.

'Let go!' Katy clung on. Ashton held the diary with one hand, and with the other shoved Katy hard. Katy's grip slipped from the book, she stumbled, tripped, and with a gasp fell backwards, her arms flailing. Sophie lunged forwards to try and grab her, but she was too far away. She had to save her friend!

In an instant, she remembered the leaf that she'd stopped from falling, frozen in mid-air.

'Earth, water, wind and fire, *hold* her!' she gasped. She shut her eyes and tensed every muscle in her body in concentration. A person was an awful lot heavier than a leaf. She had no idea if the spell would work.

Sophie slowly opened one eye, then the other.

Katy was floating on her back, just above the ground, swaying gently as if she were lying in the sea. Thank goodness she was hidden from the rest of the school by the velvet curtains. Her eyes were still wide open as she stared back at Sophie. Sophie relaxed, and Katy sank gently to rest on the stairs.

Sophie slumped against the banister with a gasp of relief.

Ashton spun round to Sophie, his eyes popping with shock.

'It's you!' he shouted.

He lunged for her. Sophie dodged him, ran for the stairs, leapt over Katy and landed at the bottom. She picked herself up and sped, pushing through the dancing crowd, towards the double doors. She slammed through them, letting them swing wildly behind her, and shot down the corridor. Behind her, she heard the doors bang open again as Ashton and Katy followed her. She skidded round a corner and found herself running towards the main kitchen. She raced inside and nearly bumped into the big fridge, knocking some of the cook's fridge magnets off as she grabbed it to steady herself. She caught her balance and rushed on, past the range and the stainless steel work tables, saw the kitchen door coming up ahead and yanked it open. Panting for breath, she hurled herself through the door, past the bins and into the courtyard. She glanced behind her – Ashton and Katy were nowhere in sight. But before she had a chance to relax, she heard someone shriek, 'Watch out!'

Sophie looked in front of her just in time to cannon head-on into two adults. She stumbled backwards, winded, on to the grass.

'Where are you going in such a rush?' a man's voice demanded from above her.

Sophie didn't reply, as she caught her breath. At least Ashton and Katy couldn't get her in front of witnesses.

'I'm really sorry,' she began, looking up. Her voice died away as she found herself looking into the scarred face of Mrs Gibson.

'You should take better care.' Mrs Gibson rubbed her arm.

From behind her, Mr Gibson added, 'You could have hurt yourself, rushing around like that.'

'Are you OK?' asked Mrs Gibson.

Sophie looked back and forth between them. Of course, she realised, they weren't here because of her. They didn't know she was a witch. They were here to give Katy a telling off.

'S-sorry,' she gasped. She got to her feet and was about to run when she heard the school doors burst open and footsteps racing towards her. Ashton's furious voice yelled, 'That's her! Mum – Dad – that's the witch!'

Sophie spun round in terror. Ashton was heading towards her, followed by Katy. She backed away and bumped into Mr Gibson. She tried to edge around him, but Mrs Gibson blocked her path.

Ashton and Katy came to a breathless halt in front of her. Katy bent over to get her breath, but Ashton took Sophie's arm and forced her to face his parents.

'Looks like Katy's been hanging out with witches instead of catching them,' he panted. 'Isn't this witch your best friend, Katy?'

Katy gulped air and nodded, but reached for Sophie's hand and held it tight.

Sophie desperately tried to look into Katy's eyes, but Katy was resolutely looking at the floor.

'Are you sure? Have you done the tests?' Mr Gibson snapped.

'No, Father. I'm sorry.' Ashton hung his head. 'I only

just found out, right this minute. She had me totally fooled.'

'Did you locate her Source, at least?' Mr Gibson asked.

Ashton said nothing.

Sophie looked down at her hand and noticed that her ring had gone. *Where could it be?* She had it when she got dressed for the dance.

'Must I do everything myself?' Mrs Gibson spat. Snapping open her handbag, she dipped her fingers into an inside pocket. She briskly tossed a pinch of iron filings at Sophie. Sophie shut her eyes, not wanting to see the moment of truth as the iron filings curved into a crescent moon. She waited for the Gibsons to grab her but they didn't. She opened her eyes again and saw the iron filings lying scattered and motionless on the ground. She stared at them in disbelief.

In the silence, Ashton spoke up. He sounded shaken.

'But – she *is* a witch. We saw her do magic. Didn't we, Katy?'

'Well, Katy?' said Mr Gibson.

For a second, Sophie thought Katy wasn't going to answer. Then, she spoke.

'No, obviously not,' she said, giving her parents a hard stare. 'Um – everyone knows there's no such thing as witches. Right, Sophie? Ashton, you need your head examined.'

There was a tense silence. Then Mrs Gibson coughed and turned to Ashton.

'Right. Right! Obviously, there's no such thing as witches. Obviously!' She gave Sophie a wide smile. 'I must apologise for my son. He gets these silly ideas . . . '

Sophie nodded speechlessly. She glanced down at the iron filings. Mr Gibson hastily stepped forward, and kicked them into the grass.

'But—' Ashton began.

'No buts!' Mr Gibson raised his voice. 'And I'm stopping your allowance. Hopefully that will teach you not to make up ridiculous stories and call people hurtful names. Witch indeed!' He laughed, and Mrs Gibson and Katy quickly joined in.

Ashton opened his mouth again, but Mrs Gibson grabbed his shoulder and steered him away. Mr Gibson followed. 'I don't know what got into you ... stupid thing to say ...'

Sophie breathed out in relief. She was safe. She wasn't going to be killed by the hunters.

She turned to Katy. 'But ... I don't understand. How come the filings didn't work? And what happened to my ring?'

Katy held out her hand in a fist and opened it. There lay Sophie's ring.

'I took it when I grabbed your hand just now,' she said. 'Remember I told you I was good at slipping jewellery off people?'

Sophie mouth fell open.

'I just didn't want my parents to see your Source,' said Katy. 'Now look in your pocket.'

Sophie stuck her hand into her jacket pocket. She felt something cold and metallic and drew out a small plastic shape of the Sphinx, with the words *Happy Holidays* written across it. She turned it over and saw the magnet on the back.

'I nicked one off the fridge as we went through the kitchen.' Katy smiled. 'I was worried that Ashton might try the iron filings test, so I dropped it in your pocket at the same time I took your ring.'

Katy held out the ring. Sophie took it and placed the magnet in her hand. She slid the ring back on her finger.

Sophie took a moment before she was able to speak. 'You lied to your parents for me. And you saved my life,' Sophie said. She could still hardly believe it. 'Even though you knew I was a witch. Thank you so much, Katy.'

'You saved mine first. You stopped me from falling and you risked your own life to do it. Even though you knew I was a witch hunter.' Katy smiled at her. 'It's me who should be thanking you.'

She opened her arms, and Sophie instinctively stepped in for a hug.

'I can't believe I'm lucky enough to have such a good friend,' Katy said. She sounded close to tears. Sophie pulled away, quickly.

'Katy,' she said, 'before you say anything else, I have

to talk to you about something. It's very important.'

'Anything.'

Sophie swallowed. 'It's my father ... he's been missing for ten years.' She saw sympathy on Katy's face, and hurried on. 'You see, I think your parents drove him away. I think they might even have killed him.'

Katy frowned. 'What was his name?'

'Franklyn Poulter.'

Katy's eyes widened and she stepped back.

'Franklyn *Poulter*? That's your dad?'

Sophie nodded. 'Why? What is it? What's happened to him?' She felt herself trembling. 'Is he ... dead?'

'No! I'm just ... startled.' Katy shook her head. 'Sophie ... your father is famous. He's one of the most powerful witches there are. My parents almost captured him but he escaped.'

'So he's alive?' Sophie realised she was clenching her hands into tense fists.

'Oh, yes! The witch hunters are still searching for him. They wouldn't be doing that if they thought he was dead.'

Sophie nodded, relaxing. There was a chance, then,

that she might find him one day – if the witch hunters didn't get to him first.

'I'll do whatever I can to help you find him,' Katy said, as if she were reading Sophie's thoughts. 'I owe you.'

Sophie smiled at her. 'Thank you. That means a lot to me.' She paused. 'You know . . . it sounds crazy, but even though our families are so different . . . I'd like to be friends. Real friends. Best friends.'

Katy smiled, her green eyes warm. 'I don't think that's crazy. I'd like that too.'

From the school building, the sounds of the dance floated across the lawns towards them. The sea beyond the cliffs glinted in the setting sunlight and Turlingham Academy had never looked so pretty. Katy stretched out her hand and Sophie took it. As they shook, her crescent moon ring flashed in the light of the sun.

'Friends for ever?' Katy asked.

Sophie squeezed her hand. 'Always.'

She had no idea how a witch and a witch hunter were going to survive, side by side, but she had a feeling that if anyone could pull it off, she and Katy could.

Just wait until I tell Callum! she thought, then stopped herself. She couldn't possibly tell Callum anything – not about Katy, or her grandmother, or her missing dad who was a famous witch.

'This is the strangest start to the term I've ever had,' she murmured, as she and Katy wandered back towards the school dance.

Katy laughed. 'And it's only just begun,' she said, as Gally leapt down from a tree branch and settled on Sophie's shoulder. She tickled her familiar under the chin.

Life at Turlingham Academy was never going to be the same again.

Want to read more?

Turn the page for a sneaky peek at book two:
Undercover Magic . . .

Sophie Morrow groaned and pulled the duvet over her head as the house filled with clattering and noise. There was no way it was time to get up!

'It's Sunday, Mum!' she called through a huge yawn. 'Go back to bed!'

The noise continued and Sophie realised it wasn't her mother moving about. It was someone hammering on the front door.

She scrambled up, dragging a hand through her messy hair, and ran downstairs. A familiar face was pressed against the frosted glass panel.

'Katy!' She flung it open. Her best friend grinned at

her, pale cheeks flushed with the autumn chill and her black hair half-hidden under a woolly hat.

'Sophie, come on out!' she said. 'The last of the leaves finally fell off the trees last night and we're mucking round in them – Callum's there!' She blushed. 'Oh, and some of the other boys are, too.'

'Cool! Give me a second to get dressed.' Sophie turned, but Katy caught her arm.

'Wait . . . I made you a little present,' she said, reaching into her coat pocket. 'I'd really like you to wear it.'

She handed Sophie a friendship bracelet, plaited together with a rainbow of coloured threads. Charms in the shape of flowers and fruit were worked into it – an ivy leaf, a bunch of cherries and a cute red tomato.

Sophie drew in her breath. 'Oh, Katy, thanks!' She laid it against her wrist, so the charms caught the light.

'You like it?' Katy asked.

'Like it? I love it!' Sophie stroked the ivy leaf. 'And the charms are perfect. Did you choose leaves and fruit because . . . ?' She tailed off, not wanting to mention the word *magic* aloud, just in case someone was listening.

Katy nodded. 'Because of your . . . green fingers.' Their eyes met and Sophie knew they were both thinking the same thing: Sophie was a witch, and witch powers came from the great forces of nature.

'It's the best present in the world,' she said, throwing her arms round Katy.

'Well, you're the best friend in the world, so you deserve it!' Katy said with a laugh. 'I made one for me, too, exactly the same.' She held up her wrist.

'So cool!' Sophie clapped her hands. 'It's like we're twins.' She noticed Katy's cheeks flush. 'I mean, obviously we look totally different and, um, our families are sworn mortal enemies, but, y'know . . .'

They laughed together. Katy came from a family of witch hunters. They'd only found out how different they were after they'd become friends, and now nothing was going to become between them – not even witch hunting.

'The bracelets aren't identical,' Sophie added,

examining the bracelets side by side. 'Yours hasn't got this bunch of cherries—'

'Oh! I almost forgot,' Katy took Sophie's friendship bracelet and flipped it over so the charms were reversed. The bunch of cherries had a piece of metal attached to the back. 'This one's special – it's really a fridge magnet.'

'Katy, that's so clever,' Sophie exclaimed, realising what it meant. Magnets blocked a witch's powers, making Sophie just like any other human. If she wore it one way, it was just a pretty bracelet. As soon as the magnet came in contact with her skin, it could save her life.

'When the bracelet's reversed, your powers will be hidden from any witch hunter,' Katy said. She hesitated, then added: 'Even my family.'

'Thanks, Katy!' Sophie hugged her again. It wasn't easy being best friends with a witch hunter – if Katy's family ever found out Sophie was a witch, they would both be in danger. But it was worth the risk, she thought. *I've never had a better friend.*

'You're welcome.' Katy hugged her back. 'Now hurry

up and get dressed so we can go and find the others!'

Sophie raced up the stairs to her bedroom, the charms on the bracelet catching the dim sunrays as she went.

*

Sophie followed Katy past the big windows of the new science block and into the courtyard. Turlingham School loomed above them, turrets and towers casting spiky shadows across the concrete. She saw her friends on the other side of the courtyard, shouting and laughing as they chased after Mark, who was carrying Erin in a piggyback across the grass, weaving in and out of the trees.

'Mark, slow down!' Erin shrieked in her American accent, between giggles. 'You're going to drop me, I swear!' The gulls overhead echoed her squeals.

'Hey, Soph!' Tall, curly-haired Callum waved to her. Sophie waved back. She'd known Callum for what seemed like for ever – her mother and his father were joint head teachers at Turlingham Academy.

'Look! No hands!' Erin yelled, waving to Sophie – then she lost her balance and slid off into a big pile of leaves with a whoop of laughter. Mark fell down next to her. Sophie ran over to them as the others crowded round, giggling and tossing armfuls of leaves on top of Erin and Mark.

'Hey, you two, stop kissing under there!' Kaz laughed as she chucked some more.

'Yeah, can't you keep your hands off each other for a second?' Katy added as she and Sophie reached them.

Sophie laughed. She knew Erin loved to be the centre of attention with Mark – and Erin seemed so happy to be finally going out with him!

Mark scrambled up out of the leaves, blushing and frowning.

'Hey, Mark, are you OK?' Sophie asked. 'We were only joking . . .'

'Yeah, course I'm OK!' Mark muttered. He ran off and joined the other boys who were hanging out under the trees.

'Oh no, did we upset him?' Lauren said, looking worried. 'We didn't mean to!'

Erin got to her feet, her cheeks red with embarrassment. 'The thing is,' she whispered, beckoning the girls in, 'don't tell him I told you, but . . . we haven't actually kissed yet.'

'Wha-at?' Kaz's mouth dropped open. 'But he's so into you!'

'Yeah!' Joanna looked puzzled. 'And you've been going out for a whole two weeks!'

'I know.' Erin's mouth turned down. 'I'm worried he doesn't like me any more.'

'As if!' Sophie replied. 'Erin, he's head over heels. Anyone can see that.'

'I hope you're right.' Erin sighed.

'We are! Come on – you're not allowed to mope about something so silly,' Sophie said, putting on a stern voice. 'Or you'll get . . .' she ducked to scoop up an armful of leaves, '. . . leaf bombed!' She hurled them at Erin, who shrieked and laughed and tried to hide behind Katy. Sophie dodged as Erin scooped up more to fight back with – and gasped as Lauren cheekily tossed handfuls over her head.

Kaz grabbed a big bunch of leaves and darted over

to the group of boys. Before Callum could react, she shoved them down the back of his jumper.

'Urgh! I'll get you for that!' Callum roared in mock anger. He scooped up more leaves and flung them at Kaz, who squealed in delight. Then a gust of tangy, salty wind blew in from the sea and suddenly all the leaves were swirling and dancing round.

Sophie grabbed some leaves out of the air, ran over to the boys and flung her armful at them.

'Girls against boys – leaf wars!' she cried.

'You're on!' Oliver Campbell, a quiet boy with a big, friendly smile, dashed forward and threw more leaves at Kaz. The others joined in.

'Oh no, I'm getting out of here!' Lauren giggled. She ducked for shelter behind the biggest oak tree. Kaz and Oliver dived round to join her.

Sophie looked up into the maze-like branches of the oak tree and saw a flash of glossy black fur. It was Gally – her squirrel familiar. She winked at him, and Gally, catching on at once, darted round the tree, shaking the branches. Kaz, Lauren and Oliver yelled as they were covered in leaves.

'Oh, look at that squirrel! It's so close!' Oliver shouted, pointing as Gally scampered away like a streak of black lightning. Kaz and Oliver chased after him, but Gally disappeared into the woods.

Sophie watched, laughing.

Katy nudged her. 'Hey – it wasn't *you* who made the leaves fall last night, was it?' she whispered, her eyes wide.

Sophie laughed again and shook her head. 'I wish my powers were that strong!' she whispered back. 'Nope, it's not magic – just autumn, same as every year.'

'Let's go and explore the woods!' Kaz yelled in the distance. The others followed her towards the trees that bordered the school.

Sophie held Katy back, and they brushed the leaves off each other. Looking up, Sophie noticed that Callum was still there, shifting from foot to foot as he gazed at Katy. 'What's up, Callum?' Sophie asked him.

'Oh . . . I – er – I just wanted to apologise to Katy for getting leaves all over her.' Callum rubbed one Converse shyly against the other.

'Oh, Callum! That's the point of a leaf battle!' Sophie teased.

Callum ignored her and came up to Katy. 'Are you OK?' he said, gazing deep into her green eyes.

Katy blushed. 'Oh . . . yeah! Of course!' She flicked a golden leaf out of her hair. 'Are you? OK, I mean?'

Sophie rolled her eyes. She wished they would just hurry up and get together. Hoping that if she left them in peace Callum would get to the point, she ran off after the others.

Sophie caught up with Kaz and noticed her glance back at Callum and Katy. Sophie's smile faltered. *Oh no, Kaz has a crush on Callum too.* But he was so obviously into Katy – in fact, he might even be making his move that very minute . . .

'So, uh, I got to level sixteen on Elfin Warriors,' Callum's voice drifted over to them, 'and now I have the secret key and forty-two extra Druid Skill Points!'

'Oh, um . . . wow,' Katy's puzzled voice replied.

Kaz looked relieved, and Sophie groaned to herself. Callum was a great friend, but he was never going to get anywhere with chat-up lines like that!

Sophie felt a pebble dig into her foot. 'Ouch! You guys go on, I'll be there in a sec,' she called.

Sophie sat down on a tree stump and began unlacing her trainer, while her friends ran on into the woods. She tipped the stone out of her shoe and sat for a moment, enjoying the still peace and the power of nature that she could feel all around her. The wind moaned through the trees and Sophie smiled to herself. But her face fell when she heard a voice from behind her.

'Nice morning for hunting witches!'

Sophie jumped up and spun round, her heart beating fast. The boy who stood scowling on the path was as handsome as Katy was pretty, and he had the same black hair and green eyes. But Sophie knew Ashton Gibson was nothing like his kind, gentle sister.

'Ashton,' she said cautiously. In the distance, she could hear her friends calling to each other as they ran through the woods. If she screamed for them, she thought, they'd come – but then Ashton would know for sure she had something to hide. He had seen her save Katy's life with a spell just a few weeks ago, and he was furious that he hadn't managed to prove to his family of witch hunters that Sophie was a witch.

Ashton stepped forward, his feet crunching in the frost. His hand was clenched in his blazer pocket.

Sophie instinctively backed away. *What's he got in there?*

He pulled out his fist, grey dust spilling between his fingers. Iron filings, the easiest way for a witch hunter to find witches. They were treated with a witch hunters' potion, designed to form into the shape of a crescent moon in the presence of a witch.

'Take that!' Ashton threw the iron filings.

Sophie barely had time to duck before the tiny pieces of iron scattered over her. Her mouth tasted sour with terror as she realised she was in big, big trouble. The iron filings fell on the floor and Sophie looked down, expecting to see the shape that would seal her fate. Except she didn't. The filings scattered and were lost on the muddy path. Sophie gasped, caught between confusion and relief.

Ashton stared at the ground, a frown of confusion

on his face. 'How the . . . ? I *know* you're a witch!' he burst out.

Sophie relaxed as she remembered her friendship bracelet. The magnet was touching her skin, protecting her.

'What do you think you're doing, Ashton?' she demanded, trying to look puzzled as well as outraged. 'First you call me a witch – that's so rude! – and then you throw stuff at me?! That could have gone in my eyes!'

Ashton's mouth hardened. 'I don't know how you're beating the test,' he said. 'But I *do* know you're a witch. I'll catch you out one day. You can't make *me* look stupid.'

He strode away.

As soon as his back was turned, Sophie checked that her friends couldn't see her from where they were and she flipped her bracelet round. She rubbed the crescent moon ring that she always wore – it was her Source, the origin of her magic. Tingling energy rushed through her, and the wind roared through the trees, as if it was strengthening her power. Silvery willow leaves swirled down and danced around her. Sophie felt a smile come to her lips as the ring glowed as pale as the frost on the ground.

'Forces of the earth,' she whispered, 'rise up!'

A huge gust of wind rushed through the clearing and tossed a huge drift of muddy leaves up into the air. Ashton cried out in disgust as they blew right into his face. He spun round, trying to beat them off, tripped on a root and went over, flailing his arms – *splash!* – into a puddle.

'You're right, Ashton – you definitely don't need me to make you look stupid!' Sophie said with a cheeky grin. Then she turned to join her friends. She didn't fancy staying round to face Ashton's anger. But as soon as she started to move, she heard a scream ring out from her left.

It was Kaz's voice – and it was the scream of someone in pain . . .